Gabriel's Vanishing Light

Kerrigan Presidents Series, Volume 4

W.J. May

Published by Dark Shadow Publishing, 2023.

This is a work of fiction. Similarities to real people, places, or events are entirely coincidental.

GABRIEL'S VANISHING LIGHT

First edition. September 15, 2023.

Copyright © 2023 W.J. May.

Written by W.J. May.

USA Today Bestselling Author
W.J. MAY

Copyright 2023 by W.J. May

GABRIEL'S VANISHING LIGHT

THIS BOOK IS LICENSED for your personal enjoyment only. This e-book may not be re-sold or given away to other people. If you would like to share this book with another person, please purchase an additional copy for each recipient. If you're reading this book and did not purchase it, or it was not purchased for your use only, then please return to Smashwords.com and purchase your own copy. Thank you for respecting the arduous work of the author.

All rights reserved. No part of this publication may be reproduced, stored in or introduced into a retrieval system, or transmitted, in any form, or by any means (electronic, mechanical, photocopying, recording, or otherwise) without the prior written permission of both the copyright owner and the above publisher of this book.

This is a work of fiction. Names, characters, places, brands, media, and incidents are either the product of the author's imagination or are used fictitiously. Any resemblance to actual person, living or dead, events, or locales is entirely coincidental. The author acknowledges the trademarked status and trademark owners of various products referenced in this work of fiction, which have been used without permission. The publication/use of these trademarks is not authorized, associated with, or sponsored by the trademark owners.

All rights reserved.
Gabriel's Vanishing Light
Book 4 of the Kerrigan Presidents
Copyright 2023 by W.J. May
Cover design by: Book Cover by Design
No part of this book may be used or reproduced in any manner whatsoever without written permission, except in the case of brief quotations embodied in articles and reviews.

Kerrigan Presidents Series

Leaders in Control
Director on a Mission
Devon Seeking Guidance
Gabriel's Vanishing Light
President on Edge
Agreeing the Future

Kerrigan Memoirs Series

The Chronicles of:
Devon
Angel
Julian
Molly
Gabriel
Rae

Have You Read the C.o.K Series?

The Prequel series is a Sub-Series of the Chronicles of Kerrigan.
The prequel on how Simon Kerrigan met Beth!!
Download for FREE:

THE CHRONICLES OF KERRIGAN: PREQUEL –
  Christmas Before the Magic
  Question the Darkness
  Into the Darkness
  Fight the Darkness
  Alone in the Darkness
  Lost the Darkness

GABRIEL'S VANISHING LIGHT

The Chronicles of Kerrigan

BOOK I - *Rae of Hope* is FREE!
Book Trailer:
http://www.youtube.com/watch?v=gILAwXxx8MU
Book II - *Dark Nebula*
Book Trailer:
http://www.youtube.com/watch?v=Ca24STi_bFM
Book III - *House of Cards*
Book IV - *Royal Tea*
Book V - *Under Fire*
Book VI - *End in Sight*
Book VII – *Hidden Darkness*
Book VIII – *Twisted Together*
Book IX – *Mark of Fate*
Book X – *Strength & Power*
Book XI – *Last One Standing*
Book XII – *Rae of Light*

THE CHRONICLES OF KERRIGAN SEQUEL
    Matter of Time
    Time Piece
    Second Chance
    Glitch in Time
    Our Time
    Precious Time

The Chronicles of Kerrigan: Gabriel

Living in the Past

Present for Today

Staring at the Future

Kerrigan Chronicles

Book 1 – Stopping Time
Book 2 – A Passage of Time
Book 3 – Ticking Clock
Book 4 – Just in Time
Book 5 – Time in the City
Book 6 – Ultimate Future

The Kerrigan Kids Series

Book 1 - School of Potential
Book 2 - Myths & Magic
Book 3 - Kith & Kin
Book 4 - Playing With Power
Book 5 - Line of Ancestry
Book 6 - Descent of Hope
Book 7 – Illusion of Shadows
Book 8 – Frozen by the Future
Book 9 – Guilt of My Past
Book 10 – Demise of Magic
Book 11- Rise of the Prophecy
Book 12 – Deafened by the Past

Find W.J. May

Website:
https://www.wjmaybooks.com
Facebook:
https://www.facebook.com/pages/Author-WJ-May-FAN-PAGE/141170442608149
Newsletter:
SIGN UP FOR W.J. May's Newsletter to find out about new releases, updates, cover reveals and even freebies!
http://www.wjmaybooks.com/subscribe

Gabriel's Vanishing Light Blurb

BE CAREFUL PULLING on threads. You never know what might unravel...

When the gang's first clue in solving Kraigan's abduction leads them to the British Museum, they think it's going to be just another mission. But as always, the 'other-Kerrigan' has some tricks up his sleeve. In an act of desperation, friends are forced to lean upon some unlikely allies, but those decisions come at a cost and the price is sometimes too much to bear.

Old assumptions are questioned and friendships are tested, as Gabriel and Devon find themselves pitted against each other on opposite sides. There are rules in place for a reason, but what happens when you bend them?

What happens when they bend so far...they break?

Chapter 1

There are some jobs, you do for money. There are some jobs, you do for morals.

There are other jobs...you do for the love of the game.

"Echo-base to team leader. Come in, team leader."

There was a whoosh of something dark—might have been shadow, might have been hair. A second later, it was whispering up the side of the museum, clinging with unnatural ease to the stone.

"...I thought *you* were team leader," it called down tentatively.

Molly shook her head in frustration, darting from topiary to topiary as she pirouetted to the front door. "I'm the renegade commander on a mission to retake my throne. Pay attention, Rae."

Devon took a deep breath, praying to the gods of patience. "Are they always like this?" he asked quietly, walking side by side with Luke. "I mean, what must it be like on actual missions? Imagine the transcripts. It's no wonder their case-officer quit."

Luke wobbled precariously beside him, five overlapping beanies stuffed atop his head. "Rudy quit because of an undiagnosed latex allergy," he replied without missing a beat. "And you're one to talk. Didn't you once sneak into an Arizona pawn shop disguised as a cactus?"

The fox cracked a reluctant grin, casting a look around the empty street. "That was Julian. I just helped him add the spikes."

"Couldn't have been me," the psychic interjected, walking brazenly down the center of the sidewalk. While the others were making at least some effort to keep to the shadows, he paced defiantly in the open air.

"That sounds like something you'd do with a *partner*—and that's not us."

Devon sent up another prayer, then jogged to catch up with him. "I thought we were past this," he coaxed. "I thought you'd forgiven me."

A frosty look passed between them.

"Did it feel like me forgiving you, when I shot you in the chest?"

On second thought, I'll keep my distance.

The fox eased backwards, rubbing absentmindedly at his sternum.

After upping their arsenal of powers by several thousand degrees, the friends had decided they wouldn't be lowering themselves through the roof after all. Nor would they be darting through a side entrance, or tunneling through the ventilation grates, or anything else that might compromise their illustrious reputation. They were the Kerrigan Gang. They'd be walking through the front door.

Or staging some kabuki theater.

"What the... what are you doing?" Devon whispered, fingers cupped around his mouth. His eyes strayed up the side of the building, barely able to distinguish the outline of his wife. She was clinging there like a gargoyle, hiccupping occasional sparks. "We decided *against* the roof, Rae."

She vanished in a *poof* of smoke, then appeared on the sidewalk beside him—cheeks flushed with excitement, tufts of oddly-colored feathers clinging to her hair.

"*You* used to see the fun in things," she accused, jabbing a playful finger into his ribs. "*You* used to tell me to enjoy the simple pleasure of my ink. Come on," she added, opening her arms as the friends ghosted up the steps, "when was the last time we did something like this together? Not since Yuri accidentally triggered that volcano—and even *that* ended with ice cream."

He opened his mouth to answer, then ended up smiling instead.

His wife had that effect on people, her husband most of all. She looked the same as the day she'd turned sixteen—brimming with energy and flushed with their latest adventure, tiny shimmers of power radiating from the magical fairy inked on her lower back. She was also taking the heist a lot better than he might have expected. They all were. Instead of berating him and Gabriel with the usual questions or judgments, they'd gotten into the spirit of things. The code-names and beanies, the quiet theme music someone had playing on their phone. Even Julian had forgotten to sulk and was playing with a signal-disruptor, shooting down the traffic cams like a cowboy in the old west.

So have some fun. Take the win.

"If you like," he whispered conspiratorially, "this can also end with ice cream."

She snorted with laughter, tossing back her long hair. "This is going to end with groveling and punishment. But I like your optimism."

They came to a stop in front of the door.

Most days, they would never consider such a direct approach. There was a reason that spies operated with discretion—there was a significantly lower chance one might get shot. But given the rather extraordinary amount of power accumulated between them, there was very little that could hamper them, and virtually nothing they couldn't achieve. Even now, they were standing in a clear patch of moonlight—trusting that between clairvoyance and the street cams, things would be fine.

"How do you want to do this?" Molly asked, somersaulting to a theatrical stop. The girl had spent the last several weeks crammed inside a remote surveillance tower, and was itching for the chance to stretch her legs. "We could melt it, incinerate it, vanish it, portal it into space. Oh, hang on!" She lifted her hands, eyes flashing with neon light. "I can just summon a little—"

"We're in downtown London," Luke inserted gently.

As the only person without ink—the one who'd been raised in a draconian monastery—it often fell on him to give his impulsive friends these little reminders. Unfortunately, they rarely listened. And he happened to be rather impulsive himself.

"Just kick it down," he concluded.

At that point, Gabriel stepped forward with a little smile.

While the others had gotten swept away in their games, he was calm and methodical—eyes flashing with cautious regularity across the empty roads, golden hair knotted practically behind his head. One hand swept over the door in a strange caress—gauging the thickness of the metal, what locks might be carved above the handle—as the other beckoned silently for Rae.

"Can you freeze whatever's on the other side?" he asked.

She glanced at the door, feeling rather deflated. No doubt she'd envisioned a cyclone, or a trebuchet, or perhaps travelling to a time before the invention of doors. But she nodded obligingly and flicked her fingers. There was a slight tightening in the air around them, like salt drying on skin.

"Done," she said softly, eyes flicking upwards. "The whole museum's locked down."

Atta girl.

"Jules?" the assassin called, glancing over his shoulder.

The psychic turned away from the street—dark hair swinging to cover his face, as his eyes glowed to life. A moment passed, and the rest of them stared. They usually stared, no matter how many times they'd seen it. Casual as it had become, it was nearly impossible to look away.

He tilted his head to the side, racing through a thousand hypothetical futures the rest of them would never know, before the glow subsided and he blinked to the present.

"We're good," Julian said.

With a little nod, Gabriel passed a hand over the door again. This time, the fox's ears perked up with a dozen metallic clicks, as the locking mechanisms slid out of place. There was a deep *crunch*, like the shifting of boulders, then the door swung open onto the steps.

The friends crowded together, peering curiously into the dark.

In those first tender years, this would have been the moment that derailed them. The breath before that first step inside, where anything in the world might happen. They'd seen rookie agents shrink back, plagued by their own superstitions and insecurities. They'd seen veteran agents make a final check with their handlers—haunted by scars of previous missions they could never take back.

But if one pushed past those initial uncertainties, broke through the crust of that fear, the opening of a door felt like standing on the edge of a great precipice. *Anything* could happen. *Anything* at all. The next adventure was just a step away, tingling at the edge of their magical fingers.

Devon took a deep breath, and stepped inside.

The museum felt entirely different without the crowds that usually filled it—hollowed and empty—like a great bell, waiting for the stick to strike. The slightest sound echoed up nine stories of marble. The grand chambers and winding corridors lay dormant and deserted, awaiting the people that would wake up in the morning and clamber inside. Despite the scale, it was almost tomblike.

Yet the friends were followed every step by a hundred pairs of watchful eyes.

"This is so creepy," Molly muttered, reaching the tip of her fingernail towards the nose of a stuffed bison. "It feels like they should lock this stuff away at night, doesn't it?"

"Why?" Luke teased, weaving an arm around her waist. "Because someone might break in?"

She considered a moment, then gave the bison a pat. "...because they might get lonely."

Rae grinned in spite of herself, studying her reflection in a Mesopotamian vase. "Those are the martinis talking," she interjected, throwing a look at her own husband. "And yes, we pre-gamed a little before coming. Not that you're in a position to judge."

"A little?" Julian muttered under his breath, lifting onto his toes to examine a reconstructed triceratops. "The guy who runs the mini-mart had to cut you guys off."

Devon pursed his lips, glancing between them.

That's why she's taking this so well.

Julian is sober. Julian shot me.

"The security guards are frozen, but I should take control of the feed." Luke hopped over a partition at the front desk, pulling a miniature disk from his pocket. He typed a few sequences into the computer, then slipped it into the drive. "That EMP you guys placed outside was adorable."

"It's standard government issue," Molly countered indignantly.

"Adorable," he repeated, eyes reflecting the glow of the screen. He typed a few seconds longer, then squinted up towards the ceiling. "Can I get a little light?"

Rae abandoned the vending machines and cupped her hands together, shaping and molding, gathering photonic particles, then she tossed a great ball of light into the air. It hovered beneath the chandelier like a miniature sun, illuminating the darkness and bringing every shadowy corner to life.

Alright, that's a nice trick.

"So what's the target?" she asked briskly, dusting off her hands. "Are we going for Persian antiquities? A Neapolitan sword? Personally, I'm hoping for something in the Egyptian wing—"

"Wait a second," Devon blurted before he could stop himself, "you don't already know?"

The words echoed over the marble as the friends came to a sudden halt.

In hindsight, he'd never know why he asked the question, why he drew the spotlight. His friends were already in the building. He could have just given them a target—trusted they would see it through. But the words flew unbidden from his lips...drawing his wife's inquisitive eyes.

"Know what?" she asked carefully, reading his every expression.

The others gathered behind her, staring as well.

For a fleeting moment, he and Gabriel locked eyes. A single, lingering glance. The kind that would sear forever into his brain. Then the assassin melted into the shadows—thanking the gods of mercy that his sister and his wife were the only people who *hadn't* come to the museum—and the fox was left to bear the weight of those eyes alone, freezing in the beam of that terrible spotlight.

Just...ease into it.

"Well to start, it isn't that big a deal," he began diplomatically, edging away from a display of Paleolithic hatchets, lest they get any ideas. "There wasn't even a reason to tell you—"

Rae crossed her arms slowly, levelling him with a cold stare. "I'm feeling less tender towards you, the longer you keep talking."

...ease into it quickly.

"A little over a week ago, I got this call. Me and Gabriel both." He resisted the urge to point, anything to divert some of the blame. "It was right after we found out about the uranium, and everything was up in the air, and we weren't even supposed to be—"

"A *lot* less tender, Devon."

There was a strangled pause.

"...it's about your brother. Half-brother."

For a single moment in time, the world and everything in it seemed to suspend. The clock stopped ticking, the wind stopped howling. The leaves on the trees hung breathless and still.

"My brother," she repeated slowly, mouth twisting with the word. "Half-brother," she corrected, before she could help herself. Her blue eyes narrowed. "What about him?"

Another pause, longer than before.

"He's been kidnapped?"

Chapter 2

"*Trespassing.*"

Gabriel sat with the others in general holding, arms resting on his knees, eyes lowered to the floor. There was a constant hum of conversation, the sudden clank of metal as someone opened a door, but for the most part, the monotony had slowed things down to a crawl.

All except Molly. She couldn't stop pacing.

"Trespassing," she said again—louder this time, in case they hadn't heard. "Can you believe that? Can you believe that *I've* been arrested for something so trivial? At this rate, we should have at least taken a souvenir from the museum. I could have fit some of those Mesopotamian necklaces in my bag…" She plopped onto a bench next to the assassin. "*Trespassing.* Kill me now."

Gabriel shrugged sympathetically. "They got Capone for tax evasion."

She shocked him in the ribs.

Unsurprisingly, it wasn't the first time she'd been incarcerated. It wasn't the first time for any of them—not by a long shot. Part of what it meant to be an intelligence operative, was to spend a not insignificant amount of time browsing the various international penal systems. Angel had once been detained for three months in a Tibetan holding facility. Julian and Devon had been caught up in a raid outside Monrovia, and found themselves carted away with the rest of the mob.

Gabriel himself had become something of a connoisseur.

He's done time for gambling in Algiers, for assault in Barcelona. He'd once turned himself over to the authorities in Singapore just to secure an asset he'd been charged with acquiring.

He'd considered blogging about it. Rae told him to get a juicer instead.

Speak of the devil...

"I can't believe I'm sitting here," she muttered, dark hair swirling like a storm cloud around her. Those blue eyes flashed to her husband, dangerous and severe. "I can't believe you got caught up in some of Kraigan's nonsense, and didn't tell anyone about it."

Devon bowed his head like a chastised schoolboy, rubbing dispiritedly at the finger-printing ink smeared over his hands. "I had Jules and Luke check up on him."

"Yeah, we said he was off the grid," Luke countered, sitting closest to the bars. "Don't try to turn this around on us. What—we didn't sleuth out your evil plot? We assumed our friends *weren't* actively keeping something from us?"

Yeah, that's right.

Molly got up calmly from the bench, and shocked Devon in the ribs as well.

"Those must be some might sharp nails you've got, little lady."

Not for the first time, the friends turned in unison to assess the people who'd been locked up with them. All of them were men. All of them were just as confused to find *women* in the general vicinity, as the officers who'd locked them up. That had been Rae's doing. Just the slightest bit of persuasion as they were being processed—mostly so she could continue yelling at her husband.

It wasn't the way things were normally done. It wasn't remotely safe for the women. At least, it wouldn't have been...if they were dealing with different women.

"Yeah, they're pretty sharp," Molly answered without missing a beat, waving her pointed manicure in the man's face. "You want to see for yourself?"

He stared a split second, then shuffled to the other side of the room.

Gabriel sighed, lowering his face into his hands.

It could have been a lot worse—he'd been expecting it to be a lot worse. The only reason they hadn't been harassed more times already, was because of their proximity to Devon—who was apparently a regular and held some degree of prestige. But he wasn't concerned with their time spent in jail. He was still back in the museum, staring at that statue and the gleaming metal underneath.

How could it have been THAT metal? How could it have been tambor?

There was movement in his periphery, as Julian sat down beside him. He studied the assassin's profile for a moment, then put a hand on his shoulder. "Hey, you doing okay?"

Gabriel startled and glanced towards him. "Sorry—what?"

The psychic tilted his head towards the door. "Try not to focus on the bars, they're just here for decoration."

The assassin stared a moment, then cracked a smile.

He'd said the same thing to Julian, the first time they'd been incarcerated together. Granted, the psychic had been in the grips of some heavy psychedelics at the time, and was firmly convinced they were standing in a swamp. The bars, he'd told Gabriel, were the least of their problems.

"I'm surprised you remember that," he answered lightly. "You were still reeling from that incident with the vending machine."

Julian blushed, but held his gaze. "Luke said it was impossible to move that statue. I could see a hundred times what would happen if you tried. You can't beat yourself up about it. This is Kraigan's mess, not yours."

It took a second to understand.

He thinks I feel guilty for failing.

For a passing moment, it was almost a humorous thought. Mostly because Julian would never use that word. He saw the potential in things—what could happen, and what could not. That was his gift. He was also sweet. No, Julian would never frame it in those terms.

Gabriel certainly would.

He'd been raised on the idea, living each moment on a razor's edge. There was no pass or fail in Jonathon Cromfield's school for misfit toys. You gave him perfection—every time—or he would find someone else who could. Gabriel hadn't been worried about the statue, or the gold, or his inability to move it. His focus had been more directed—to the material itself.

"Thanks, Jules."

The psychic studied him, then cracked a smile. "You don't give a crap about the statue."

For the second time, Gabriel looked at him in surprise. They stared at each other a lingering moment, then he shook a finger between them, like he could ward those insights away.

"Don't use that witchcraft on me. Go sit somewhere else."

Julian laughed softly and let the subject drop, trying his best to ignore the marital showdown that was happening on the other side of the cell.

"So what happened to the other envelopes?" Rae demanded, having successfully cornered her husband between the drinking fountain and a body-builder who was holding his ground.

"They were blank," Devon answered swiftly, trying to diffuse that righteous fury by being as forthcoming as possible. "Three more envelopes—all blank. We just assumed it meant we'd need to solve three little puzzles. Like this one."

"And you didn't tell me," she growled, pacing away and returning again. "My psychotic little brother gives you a treasure box, and you *didn't tell me.*"

He winced apologetically, desperate to take it back. "Little *half*-brother."

She gave him a dainty smack in the chest with enough secret force to break bones.

"How long are we going to be in here?" Molly interrupted their feud, glancing upwards with a grimace. "There's only so long I can stand under fluorescent light."

"I don't know," Gabriel interjected, suddenly desperate to get out of the grungy little building. "We haven't been allowed to make a call."

They hadn't been allowed to make a call. But someone came anyway.

And given the someone in question, the friends would rather have stayed in jail.

"Well, well, well..." Aria clapped her hands with triumphant derision, walking down the flickering hallway at a glacial pace. "How the mighty have fallen."

"IT'S JUST SO DISAPPOINTING..."

The gang was released on impressive bail, but their children would have paid it a thousand times over for the rare opportunity to savor such a blessed moment to its fullest extent. They had loudly proclaimed their parents' innocence. They had sworn by God to avenge them, voices ringing over the disinterested halls. They had driven them home with a terrifying lack of attention, forcing the older generation to sit in the back seat. When they filed into the Alden's living room, it hadn't gotten any better. They had settled to various places of attention, then Aria had risen to her feet.

Then she climbed a bit higher, standing on the coffee table instead.

"It's just so disappointing...when one of your childhood heroes..."

Gabriel lowered his eyes to the floor, letting out a tired sigh. He usually enjoyed the children's games. He usually encouraged them. But today, he was in no mood.

"I know I'm disappointed," Lily interjected quietly, meeting her father's gaze. "Not even angry, I'm just...*disappointed*."

Julian met her gaze evenly, but there was a twitch in his jaw.

"I, for one, am just glad we decided to track you," James added brightly. He'd conjured himself popcorn, and was perched high on the mantle. "We wanted to order in some pizza, but no one had remembered their cards."

"So what?" Rae countered, hands on her hips. "You were going to make us drop whatever we were doing and drive over?"

"*That's not the point, Mom!*"

"It's just so disappointing..." Aria was undaunted, locking eyes with her father, "...when one of your childhood heroes...misses the mark so completely..."

"Because you have such potential," Lily murmured, staring at her father with those prophetic eyes. "Such unbelievable potential, and to see you wasting it..." She trailed off, lifting a hand to her chest. "It *wounds* me. To some profound, unattainable, impossible-to-live-up-to—extent."

Julian's arms gripped tighter on his recliner, angled towards his daughter's across the room.

"Stop seething about the pizza, Mom," James complained, oblivious to anything else that was happening. "It's not like we wouldn't have saved you a slice."

"*That's not the point, James!*"

"Would you guys just drop it about the pizza?" Aria hissed. "I'm in the middle of my big speech." She cleared her throat, straightening up a bit higher. "As I was saying—"

"Arie, they've had enough," Jason interrupted quietly, casting a look at his father.

"No, let me finish." She cleared her throat again, almost vibrating with happiness. "It's just so disappointing...when one of your childhood heroes...misses the mark so completely...they get themselves arrested like a common criminal. Really puts things into perspective, doesn't it?"

"Trespassing?" Benji added, with a grimace of disgust. "Really, Mom?"

"I had like nothing to do with it!"

There was a ringing silence, then Lily let out the softest of sighs.

Julian rose to his feet. "I am *not* like that, Lily Elizabeth!"

"Enough," Jason repeated, pushing to his feet as well. "You owe us fifty thousand pounds. We'll take it in bank notes, or just a massive IOU. But the money would be nice," he added.

At that point, Devon took out his earbuds. "Are we done?"

They certainly were. There was only so much gloating the parents could tolerate before they started seeking vengeance, and the kids were still hunting for dinner. Already, Lily was taking a credit card from her father's wallet, slipping it into her purse with a charming smile.

Gabriel glanced curiously across the living room, as Aria hopped off the coffee table, catching the heel of her boot on the edge. Benji and Jason rushed forward to steady her, but her brother had already beaten them to it—appearing beside her and offering a steady hand.

The assassin froze a split second in surprise, then glanced across the room to where Rae and Devon had turned their attention elsewhere—forever missing the opportunity to see their children share a quiet moment of sibling togetherness. They wouldn't believe it later, when he told them.

"Hey, is everything okay?" Jason weaved towards him through the crowd, slipping his arms into the sleeves of his coat. "You look a little..." He switched paths. "What's up with the museum?"

Gabriel sighed, rubbing at his eyes. "It's a long story. Can we talk about it tomorrow?"

"Yeah, of course."

The two embraced, then parted ways at the door. The rest of them were already skipping down the driveway—sharing their favorite highlights and making plans to reenact them at the bar around the corner. James tagged along after them, conjuring himself a hasty ID.

Gabriel's lips twitched with a knowing smile, then he swung the door shut.

Home, at last.

The place felt too big without Natasha—hollow and endless, echoing with every sound. Or maybe there wasn't enough of him without her there to fill it. She soothed the aches and healed the parts that needed mending—finding the pieces that cooled too fast, and warming them back to life.

He went quickly through his nighttime routine before settling into bed. One arm reached absently over the empty sheets, as the other flung carelessly across his chest.

Five hours later, he was still staring at the ceiling.

GABRIEL CHEWED HIS *cereal slowly, depressingly aware of what was going to happen when he finished the bowl.*

There was a new hybrid in the tunnels. A shifter, from the sounds of it. The guy must have been something exotic to get Cromfield so excited, but there was no point in asking what that something might be.

He would find out soon enough. He'd been tasked with processing the man.

"Morning, kid. How was Bolivia?"

He knocked forward as a telekinetic swept into the kitchen behind him, giving him what was meant to be friendly clap on the back. A part of him was vaguely surprised. The people who worked on the lower rungs of

Cromfield's organization rarely spoke to him or Angel. He wasn't even sure of half their names—he'd learned to identify them by their tatùs instead. He was even more surprised because this was the family wing. Or at least, that was how he'd come to think of it—when he let his thoughts run away with themselves. It was directly beneath the sanctuary, a place of privilege where few people were allowed to go.

"The big man's in a fine mood this morning," the telekinetic continued, pouring himself a cup of coffee and staring at the back of the assassin's golden head. "I can't remember the last time I saw him smile."

Gabriel twisted around, unable to picture it. "What are you doing here?" he demanded bluntly. "That's Jason's mug."

Jason Archer had died almost ten years earlier. A single gunshot wound, straight to the chest. The only thing fast enough to stop the fastest man alive. According to legend, he'd wanted to go. He'd wanted to go for a long time.

Gabriel didn't believe that. He refused to throw away the mug.

The telekinetic smiled like he might be joking, then realized he wasn't and poured the coffee into the sink. He mumbled an inarticulate apology, rinsing the glass and placing it back on the shelf. There was a noise from somewhere above them. The fitted stone in the ceiling trembled with distant footsteps, raining down tiny showers of dust.

"I'd finish that cereal," the man advised, pacing back through the door. "He'll be looking for you."

Yeah, no shit.

Gabriel turned with a sigh back to the table, letting the cereal drip slowly off his spoon. It was a disgusting concoction that Angel had brought back from the 'real world.' Something that claimed to taste like every color in the rainbow, and scraped like gravel down the back of his throat. He pushed the bowl away, unable to eat another bite.

"It's going to be fine," he said aloud, trying to steady himself.

He wasn't usually involved in the processing. He was tasked with capturing the hybrids, dragging them back in chains, but what happened after they passed through the doors was none of his business. At least, that's what he told himself when he lay awake at night, trying to sleep. Of all the lies he spun, it was the most transparent.

He knew what happened to them. He could hear their screams.

The door opened again and he let out a breath, trying to rein in his anger. When that didn't work, he twisted around, setting down his spoon. "This isn't a buffet. Why don't you—"

His throat seized up with a silent gasp to see Cromfield standing in the kitchen.

"Are you hoarding the breakfast cereal?" he asked pleasantly.

Gabriel hastened to attention, pushing back his chair, but the man was too fast for him. Before he could stand, Cromfield was already behind him—resting both hands upon his shoulders.

"It's going to be an exciting morning, Gabriel. Are you ready for it?"

The assassin stiffened beneath his hands, pulling in a jagged breath. The telekinetic was wrong—this was a hell of a lot more than a good mood. The man was downright giddy. And still waiting for an answer.

He nodded quickly, eyes on the table. "Yes, sir."

Even as he said the words, the fear and dread that had plagued him all morning vanished, replaced with a steely determination to make the man proud. Whatever was demanded, he swore a silent vow to see it through.

And hated himself a little more.

"We received a gift today," Cromfield murmured, squeezing his shoulders. He didn't seem to realize he was doing it. His eyes glowed with excitement as they fixed upon the wall. "One that could change everything."

Gabriel was motionless as a statue beneath his hands, unable to remember another time the man had ever touched him. Countless times in anger, but never anything like this. His hands were so warm—he could feel it seeping into his shoulders. It was always cold in those little corridors. He and Angel were always shivering. But Cromfield was never cold, he *was always in action. Moving with great purpose, while they trailed behind him like ghosts.*

He found himself wanting to say something, wanting to prolong the conversation. Just a little bit longer. Just so he could remember the feeling after it was gone. He opened his mouth, breathless and searching.

"Finish your breakfast," Cromfield said abruptly, sweeping to the door. "I'll need you at your best."

Gabriel stared at the spot where he disappeared, waiting for his hands to stop shaking, waiting for his heart to fall back into its normal rhythm—forbidding himself to think about whatever was coming next. The second he was under control, he picked up his spoon and returned to the cereal, finishing his breakfast in throbbing silence.

He choked down every bite.

Gabriel awoke with a gasp, hands clenched into fists around the blankets.

The sky was still dark and the windows had frosted over. His breath clouded in front of him, bursting in shallow gasps. He bowed his head, repeating the same mantra as always.

"It wasn't real—that's over now. It wasn't real."

But he could still remember the warmth of the man's hand on his shoulder.

He could still remember the chill when he took it away.

Unable to stay in bed, he planted both feet on the floor and reached for his jacket. His eyes drifted automatically to the door. He climbed out the window instead.

Even in the darkness, he was sure-footed against the tiles—ghosting along to his favorite perch, with his back against the chimney. He settled down and fished a phone out of his pocket.

It rang twice.

"You miss me already?"

He closed his eyes with a smile as Angel's voice drifted across the line. "How's Angola?" he answered.

"It's about the same as the last time I came." There was a burst of gunfire, a shattering of glass. "And the time before that. And the time before that." Another spattering of bullets, and a click as she reloaded. "I'm starting to worry, I'm the common denominator."

He chuckled softly, tapping his finger against the phone. "It takes a special kind of arrogance to assume you could be the root cause for every single problem in Africa. Even I'm not that vain."

"Don't be ridiculous. I had an excellent teacher." There was an imperceptible pause, before she continued. "It's late your time. What's the matter?"

This was very like his sister. Not to ask if everything was all right, but to merely assume that something was wrong. The same ghosts that haunted him haunted her as well. But he didn't want to stir up those ghosts tonight. He just wanted to talk with his sister.

"Nothing's wrong. Just wanted to hear your voice." He drew in a slow breath. "Angie, you remember that story about the ghost and the bear? The one we said haunted the eastern corridors?"

She thought for a moment. "The one who got shingles?"

He stretched out his legs, lifting his eyes to the moon. "Tell me again..."

Chapter 3

It was still dark when Devon pulled onto the interstate, flying across the English countryside to the distant towers of Guilder. Even if the sun had risen, there was little chance it could penetrate the thick storm clouds knitted above him. It was as though the sky was at war with itself, churning and roiling and reassembling, as a heavy torrent of rain drenched the world below.

It might have been an English winter.

It might have been his passive-aggressive wife.

"Good morning, sir. You're here early."

A man waved cheerfully as he rolled to a stop at the checkpoint beside the gate—his face barely visible beneath the large scarf wrapped around it. The rain was coming down hard, but he was standing where he always stood, passing a magical hand over the hood of the car.

Toby Mackerel.

Toby's ink was two-fold: checking for danger and intent. Between that combination and the fact that he fainted at the sight of blood, the security detail had been a good fit. The only person he refused to scan was Angel. Apparently, the mere sight of her was enough to set his tatù ablaze.

"You know, we built a whole cottage just so you could do this inside." Devon lifted his chin obediently, as that hand passed over him as well. "I'd also give anything in the world for you to stop calling me sir, Toby. We cheated off each other in honors chemistry. I can't be *sir*."

"First world problems," the man answered brightly, waving him along. "And rest assured, I remember that time you nearly choked to death on pop-rocks, even when I'm calling you sir."

Devon rolled his eyes with a grin, and sailed past him.

Despite the early hour, the parking lot was already half-full when he got there—a tired mix of over-stressed teachers and agents wired for different time-zones. He waved to a few of them as he paced across the Oratory mats, before slipping through the secret passage that led to the tunnels that ran below the school. The air was cooler down there, and smelled faintly of cleanser. He slowed his pace upon discovering the tunnels were empty, wandering slowly down the unending hall.

He remembered the first time he and Julian had been allowed down there—their wide-eyed shock when the wall they'd been sparring beside for months slid open to reveal a set of descending stairs. It had been a bad day for it. There was a pair of shifters doing weight training upstairs, and the ceiling was rattling so violently, they'd been convinced the entire place was about to collapse.

It didn't help that we were hyped up on all those energy drinks—

"Hey, you look tired."

Devon jumped in his skin to discover that he wasn't alone at all. The lamps had been lit in the secretarial alcove outside his office, and a familiar face was glowering in the glow of her phone.

"Aren't you supposed to be able to sense when people are there?" she added.

He let out a slow breath, then continued forward. "Haley, you are a ray of sunshine. Has anyone ever told you that?"

She tilted her head with a sweet smile. "Not *nearly* enough." She continued texting as he fumbled around in various pockets, trying to locate his keys. The phone lowered a few inches, and she tracked his progress over the rim of the screen. After a few seconds passed, she cleared her throat. "You can use the coatrack, you know."

He glanced over, raking back loose strands of hair. "Pardon?"

"The *coatrack*"—she gestured to the antique stand behind her—"that big thing in the corner that's meant for your *coat*. You can use it, Devon. It's not like it's reserved or something."

He flashed a look over her shoulder, ready with a hundred excuses—but a single look in the corner and they died on his tongue. "That's Carter's coatrack," he mumbled, continuing his search.

He regretted saying it the moment the words passed his lips, bracing for the inevitable impact. He and Haley had never had the easiest relationship, not since their schooldays, and she would pounce on something like this. But she merely nodded, lowering the phone.

"Yeah, I get that." She considered him a moment, then reached into a drawer and pulled out a master key—tossing it across the room. "Here, you probably left it on your desk."

He caught it with a look of surprise. "Thanks, Haley."

She shrugged and popped in some earbuds. "Whatever."

Progress!

He opened the door quickly and returned the key, finding his own set lying in the center of the desk, just like she'd predicted. After securing them firmly to his house keys, he flipped on some music and reached for the pile of folders beside him, pulling the top one off the stack.

"Alright," he murmured, leaning back in his chair, "let's see what madness is brewing today..."

THREE HOURS LATER, Devon was still working on the same file.

His shoes were gone, his thermos was empty, and he was hunched immovably over the desk, reading through the dense material with a frown. It was no longer an active case file—he merely needed to sign the court transcripts and be done. But never had he read such a convoluted tale.

...at which point, the defendant burst into song...

The door flew open, and he startled with a gasp.

"Good morning," he said as Gabriel stormed inside, flinging down his jacket on one of the open chairs. There was a rigid tension to every movement, and sleepless bruises under his eyes. The fox set down the papers slowly, staring up from the desk. "What happened to you?"

The assassin merely shook his head.

"Is there any coffee?" he asked quietly.

"Here, you can have some of mine." Devon pulled a mug from the cabinet and reached for his thermos, before remembering he'd emptied it an hour before. "Actually, I think it's—"

"Doesn't matter."

The fox watched as he settled at the desk, reaching without thinking to correct the angle of his picture frames. He'd never noticed the assassin's obsessive-compulsive tendencies until his wife had pointed them out one day—remarking on the way Gabriel always had to straighten his chair when leaving a table. Since then, it had become an absentminded pastime, trying to figure them out.

The assassin knocked four times on a door, never three. He checked the burners on a stove each time when passing, always glanced towards the exits before turning off a light.

Back in the old days, Devon used to play games to test him—leaving cabinet doors open and knocking the furniture crooked when he walked past. Then one afternoon, Gabriel had walked in on him mislabeling the spice rack. The retaliation had been epic. The fox had nearly lost a tooth.

"So now that we've dealt with this Kraigan business—do you want to pick one of these assignments?" he offered, waving the same paper he'd shown their friends a day before. A shopping list for those interested in creating a supernatural shadow-organization. "The office pretty much ran itself while we were in Texas. I think it's safe to assume we can take something off the list."

Gabriel's eyes flashed up for a brief moment before returning to the desk. "We made the list," he answered tersely.

Right.

"Okay, well...there's an old stockpile of inhibitors they might go after in Prague," Devon suggested lightly, scanning down the page. "They're missing the base fluid, but it isn't that hard—"

"Fine," Gabriel said shortly. "Whatever you want."

Devon's eyes flew up, but after so many years, he knew better than to engage.

Despite his more theatrical tendencies, the assassin was a bulwark—a pillar of strength and consistency the fox had leaned on many times himself. It wasn't that he was inherently stable, he'd simply grown up in a whirl of such chaos, he had learned it was sometimes better to keep still.

But there were times when that endless poise got away from him, when that composure stretched thin enough to reveal the cracks just underneath. And the flaming temper beneath that.

Devon knew better than to engage. But he sometimes couldn't help himself. "So I noticed you tense up a little at that tambor stuff," he began casually, playing with the edges of the paper as he cast secret glances across the desk. "What is it?"

The assassin merely shrugged. "It's a rare metal. Like I told you."

The fox tilted his head, trying to catch his eyes. "There must be more to it than that—"

"Fine," Gabriel snapped, "you got me. I've seen it before." He put down the file he'd been holding, glaring openly across the desk. "You know what, Devon? You should be a spy."

The words hung in the air between them as the clock ticked loudly on the wall. The seconds dragged past in cold silence, one after another, until the assassin finally returned to his work.

Devon let out a quiet breath, released from that arctic gaze.

He'd been the one to initiate, he knew this. He'd been the one to press. But the longer they sat in that suffocating silence, a seething frustration boiled in his veins.

Why must it always be like this? Why must things always be difficult?

His eyes drifted sideways, finding the assassin's inscrutable face.

How are we supposed to do this together, when every time something unexpected happens, the guy abandons all civility and turns into a raging—

"I'm getting some more coffee," he announced without warning. "You want a cup?"

Gabriel shook his head, eyes on his laptop.

Good.

The fox was already pushing to his feet, sliding his arms into the sleeves of his jacket. It was still pouring outside, he could hear the patter of raindrops even so far beneath the ground, but he decided to head to the cafeteria anyway. Better to get a little distance; anything was better than this.

"I'll be back in a few," he said distractedly, pacing across the room. "Then we can contact the Prague office and start making arrangements for..."

He trailed off as the door swung open, revealing a mob of thirty angry people standing on the other side. For a split second, they looked just as surprised to see him.

Then a shifter in the front stepped forward. "Why didn't you tell us?" he demanded.

Devon stared at him in shock, while Gabriel stood up slowly behind him. "Tell you what?" he asked incredulously.

There was a quiet hiss in the crowd behind them, like someone had poured cold water over a flame. It spread from person to person, growing louder and louder, before flying back in his face.

"That the renegade shadow organization we've been chasing, the one who broke into a PC lab and stole the makings of a nuclear warhead...they're all Xavier Knights."

"THEY'RE *not* Xavier Knights." Devon raised his hands in the air, doing his best to silence the crowd.

When the office had filled to the point of asphyxiation, he and Gabriel had moved to the Oratory, searching for air to breathe and a discreet exit in case things went south. Of course, they'd forgotten to take into account the domed ceiling—magnifying even the slightest sound and flinging it back at them tenfold. They'd also forgotten about the weapons rack in the corner.

"Let me be clear," the fox repeated himself, speaking slowly. "The men and women we're after are *not* Xavier Knights. Not anymore. From what I've come to understand, they broke with the agency some time ago and haven't been heard from since. Are you listening to me?" he pressed a bit sharply, looking from person to person. "They in *no way* speak for our friends at the Abbey."

There was history enough between the two agencies without adding the word *nuclear*.

At present, things had never been better. They'd never been more closely entwined. But that was a two-way road. And it took only a spark for such competition to ignite into something more.

"But our *friends at the Abbey* didn't tell us about this!" a curly-haired conjurer shouted in reply, twisting his own phrase against him. "We only found out about their little uprising when it broke into one of our research facilities, and wheeled the makings of a warhead out the front door!"

Voices called out in agreement, catching like wildfire.

"*Who knows if they would have said anything if we hadn't found out ourselves!*"

"Something as big as all that—and they keep it from us!"

"Why stop there? What else aren't they saying?"

"How could *you* not tell us?" a voice called from the back.

Devon glanced up to see a shifter standing amongst the others, arms folded angrily across his chest. He transformed into something huge and improbable—a lion, or a mammoth, or something else the fox always managed to forget. A nice enough guy when you caught him alone, but he was a brawler at heart and was always one wrong breath away from a fight. Already, he could see the veins jutting out from his neck and his fingers curling to attention, as he waited for a reply.

"I don't know, Raul," Gabriel snapped. "All signs point to: you would take it really well."

While the fox had been attempting to soothe the riotous crowd, the assassin seemed only to resent them—leaning broodingly against the railing with both arms folded over his chest. At several points, Devon had glanced back at him for assistance. It had yet to arrive.

"Devon," a quieter voice echoed, "how could you not tell us?"

It might have been the person who said it, or merely the softer tone. But the question landed differently than the others, catching the fox's ear. His eyes searched through the crowd, alighting on a pint-sized telepath he'd trained himself. They lingered there, wide and considering.

"Maybe I should have," he murmured, shaking his head. One by one, the people around them fell silent. "Maybe things would have been better if I did." He shook his head again, gazing around the room. "Or maybe I was worried something like this might happen," he added a bit louder. "Maybe I felt too bloody hypocritical—with the voice of Clifford Barnes ringing in my ears."

Not a single word was spoken. The place was as quiet as a grave.

"Those people have stood by us when they didn't have to," Devon continued, stepping off the bleachers so he was even with the crowd. "They've come to our aid time and time again—seeing us through the likes of Victor Mallins, of Jonathon Cromfield." Each name rang out in the silence, lodging like a blade. "I haven't come so far, only to turn my back on the people who've helped me. I haven't been through so much to not know the difference between my enemies and my friends."

He opened his mouth to say something further, then merely shook his head.

"The Knights didn't ask for our help," he concluded softly, "they didn't have to. We're going to stand beside them. And if anyone has a problem with that...there's the door."

Please, don't open the door.

There was a terrifying moment when he thought they would. A hundred sets of eyes locked on his face, and he could almost see the gears turning as they made up their minds. Then at no signal that he could discern, they nodded their agreement and returned to their training—falling into the same trusted rotations they'd performed a thousand times before.

Devon stood there without moving, heart pounding in his chest.

He kept waiting for something to happen, for something to go wrong. But fast as they'd come together, they just as quickly dispersed. When the last of them cleared, he saw a lone man standing by the double doors. A man he just realized had been standing there for quite some time.

Crap.

"Gabriel," he said quietly, drawing the assassin's eye.

No one dared to speak as Anthony Fodder made his way slowly across the mats, walking with such steady confidence, you'd never think the room had just been echoing with cries of revolt.

He came to a stop in front of them, regarding each one in turn. "That was a nice speech, Wardell."

Devon blushed to the roots of his hair, wishing they'd stayed in the office. "You weren't supposed to hear it," he replied.

The commander merely nodded. "We need to talk."

"THIS IS TURNING INTO a disaster." Fodder pressed the secret lever himself and led the way into the corridors, nodding a curt greeting to the secretaries, before hanging up his coat on the rack. Once they stepped into the office, he pushed a button on the wall, and an antique fireplace sprang suddenly to life.

Devon and Gabriel froze behind him.

I thought that was decorative.

"Do you hear me?" the commander repeated. "A complete disaster."

He settled not at the desk like they'd been expecting, but into one of the leather recliners that had been angled beside the hearth. Devon paused again, feeling suddenly off-balanced. He wondered if that was where he and Carter had conducted their business. He could easily imagine them sitting there—balancing the world's problems, with a glass of aged whiskey in their hands.

He and Gabriel shared a quick look, then dragged their own chairs to join him.

"I thought it passed disaster when things went nuclear," the assassin replied conversationally.

Oh, NOW you speak.

"But that's part of the problem." Fodder listened a moment, as if checking the hallway, then leaned intently forward, arms on his knees. "I've been over and over the security footage. I've gone through the interrogation transcripts. I've even had Luke dig through the archives on the off-chance there was something we missed." He paused, drawing in a breath. "There's simply no earthly reason that the people in question would be reckless enough to steal from a PC base."

Devon crossed his legs, trying to match the man in gravitas. Trying and failing. Gabriel cocked a sarcastic eyebrow, and he put both feet back on the floor.

"It sends a message," he offered.

"But they aren't trying to send a message," Fodder answered. "They're trying to start their own organization—and the first step in that process is not pissing off one of the biggest games in town. I mean, I knew they were resentful, but I never imagined they would do something like that."

The fox looked at him suddenly—struck by something in his tone, in the tired lines around his eyes. For the first time, he realized how very painful this must be. Forget breaking and entering, the man's own people had gone missing. Some of them he'd probably known since they were sixteen. Or even younger than that. The Knights had been raising and sheltering whole families with ink since long before the PC allowed its members to share the secret. In a way, they were more of a true community than the people at Guilder had ever truly managed to achieve.

He flushed with guilt at not having thought of it sooner. That wasn't idle speech-making about Clifford Barnes. He still felt the sting of that betrayal every day.

"That isn't the only problem," Gabriel inserted quietly. "I don't care if they were never intending to use it, if I went through the trouble of stealing a canister of uranium, there's no way in hell I'd leave it in a storage locker on the side of the road."

The commander nodded slowly, eyes fixed upon the fire. "It doesn't make any sense," he murmured. "These are well-trained people. *Smart* people. There has to be something else going on. Something that's driving them to...but I can't see it." He leaned back with a weary sigh, rubbing the bridge of his nose. "I'm usually able to see it."

Devon froze in his chair, unsure what to say.

It wasn't boasting or false-confidence. The Knights' commander was a living legend. If there was a piece missing from their puzzle, there's no one in the world he'd trust more to find it. But in all the years they'd known each other, he'd never seen this side of him. Tired and uncertain. It was a glimpse behind the curtain he would never have believed, if it wasn't right there in front of him.

Not until later did he understand, it was one of the greatest compliments he'd ever receive.

"The people who left," he prompted. "I'm assuming they were employed by the agency?"

Fodder nodded briskly. "I already had Jeremy send over the files. They were good, some of my best. People I'd have trusted with my life. But they were never..." He paused, considering. "They were never content with the way things were. They were always looking for something bigger, something better."

Gabriel tilted his head with a wry smile. "Looks like they found it."

Devon flashed him a look, resisting the urge to kick him under the chair. But it didn't seem to matter. The commander merely nodded as though he was probably right.

"We need to find *them*," he concluded, suddenly businesslike. "Have your people review the files, then we can cross-reference points of interest. Safe-houses, aliases. The usual. Once you're finished, I'll have my secretary call to schedule a—"

"*This is unbelievable!*"

The door flew open again as James stormed into the room—as oblivious to the confidential meeting, as he'd been to the large group of people that had congregated upstairs. He marched right past the fireside chat and perched on the edge of his father's desk, arms fiercely folded. When the trio did nothing but stare back in silent astonishment, he rolled his eyes with a sarcastic prompt.

"Isn't anyone going to ask me what's wrong?"

There was a beat of silence, then Devon half-pushed from his chair, as confounded as he was utterly embarrassed. "Jamie, we're in the middle of—"

"I can't do my dive certification in Fiji because the swells are too high after a tropical storm," the boy announced, as if they'd been waiting for the information. "Yeah—*I know.*"

...what?!

Fodder leaned back in his chair, templing his fingers with a smile. "Nothing like a drive across town to put things in perspective."

"Bloody hell," Devon cursed under his breath, ignoring the way Gabriel was shaking with silent laughter behind him. "James, I'm *working.* This isn't the time."

"This is time-sensitive," the boy countered evenly, holding his ground. "The plane leaves in an hour, Dad. I need you to call the diving instructor—tell him it's fine."

Devon nodded quickly, waving him to the door. "Alright, just give us a second to..." He caught himself just as fast. "It's *not* fine, Jamie. He's the expert, not me. If he says it's too dangerous—"

"We do more dangerous stuff than that all the time," James complained, slipping into that particular tone only a teenager could ever achieve. "I need this certification so I can go with Emma and her friends over spring break. If I don't leave now—"

"I already said you were staying in London over spring break," Devon hissed, unable to believe they were actually having the discussion. He took a breath for patience, hyperaware of the men watching on either side. "One way or another, if there was a storm, then I can't—"

"Ugh, fine. I'll go ask someone else."

Like who?!

James hopped off the counter with a scowl, taking time to straighten his jacket, before noticing the unexpected visitor by the fire. "Oh, hey, commander. I'm digging the tie."

"Thank you, Jamie. You heading off?"

"Apparently, I am," the boy answered with another vicious scowl. He leveled it squarely at his father. "*Apparently*, I need to find someone who can reverse the damage of a tropical storm."

He was gone before anyone could speak, slamming the door behind him.

Devon stared in silence—unable to believe it had happened, unable to think of a single thing he could say in reply. After a few seconds, the commander did it for him.

"Things you learn when you're a parent: you're responsible for the weather."

The fox grimaced apologetically. "In that regard, my wife has a slight upper hand."

To his extreme surprise, Fodder actually started chuckling—pushing to his feet. "Sometimes, I wonder what it must be like at your dinner tables. Then I decide I probably don't want to know."

Devon smiled in return, standing up beside him.

In a way, he was grateful for the ease of the exit. If he'd been given more time to consider, he probably would have sent the commander on his way. But he found himself saying a final thing.

"You understand why we can't back off?" he asked abruptly, causing the man to pause at the door. "One of our men died, Andrew. I know this involves one of your financiers, and I apologize for that, but there isn't—"

"There's no apology necessary," Fodder cut him off briskly. "If I was in your position, I'd be saying the same thing." He paused a moment, assessing him. "You know, your father-in-law is back in town. We had dinner the night before last."

"Yeah, I saw him. You planning to go into retirement too?"

"And miss out on all this?" Fodder flashed a wry smile, but he paused again with his hand on the door. "Devon, whatever their crimes, whatever their reasons...those are still my people out there. If there's even the slightest chance I can get some of them back...I'm taking it."

Devon nodded slowly, weighing his next words. "I sincerely hope that works. But if it doesn't...?"

The words trailed off, as each of them filled in the rest. It was quiet a few seconds, then the commander stepped forward and shook each of their hands in turn.

"Let's hope it doesn't come to that," he concluded.

He left not long after—bidding farewell to the secretaries, and heading off down that long and imposing hall. The others stared after him, watching from the doorway.

After a long stretch of silence, Gabriel flashed a tight grin.

"That went well."

Devon scowled, stalking off down the hall. "Coffee...I need bloody strong coffee..."

THE SUN WAS JUST REACHING its peak when Devon pushed out of the Oratory and drew in a breath of clean air. It had finally stopped raining, but the air was still thick with moisture and the ground smelled rich and wet. He took another breath, making a silent vow to relocate his office outside, then headed towards the cafeteria—only to see a familiar face coming up the path.

"Hey," he said in surprise, "aren't you supposed to be in Angola?"

Angel ignored the question, gesturing to the doors. "Is Gabriel in there?"

"Yeah, he's been a little..." He trailed into silence, deciding it probably wasn't best to finish that sentence. "What are you doing back so soon?" he repeated his original question. "I thought it was going to take another week to get the code."

She tossed him a hunk of twisted metal. "This was faster. But I was hoping to ask you—"

"Is this a *bomb*?"

The conversation screeched to a halt as they both stared at the dilapidated contraption in his hands. At that point, it looked like more a microwave had lost a fight with a blender, but he could still make out a faded serial number etched into the side.

A pair of freshmen startled at the word, quickening their pace as they hurried by.

"A dismantled bomb," Angel corrected, flashing a sweet smile. "Do you want to grab a late dinner tonight? I'm still on West African Standard Time, but there's a new Thai place I'd love to—"

"Stop that," Devon said through clenched teeth, cradling the mangled device.

"...what?"

"Stop trying to be charming. Stop trying to get me to like you."

Strangely enough, it wasn't the first time it had happened. She had tried to do it once before, announcing it at the gang's last Christmas party with a poison smile. She was going to smother their blood feud. Smother it in love. The rest of the friends had cheered, dabbing away festive tears.

Devon had screamed and thrown her drink in the fire.

She let out a theatrical sigh and planted a hand on her hip, shaking her head like he was being very silly. "Alright, why is it so hard to believe—"

"I can't," he interrupted, holding up a hand, "I can't do this today, Angel. I'm still waiting to hear back from three recon teams, we narrowly avoided an inter-agency bloodbath, and my son is going to hex me for not changing the weather patterns in Fiji. I'm also *dangerously* low on coffee."

There was a pause.

"...I can get you a coffee."

"I can order your death and claim it was a typo."

The two lapsed into silence, testing each other's resolve.

The last time, he hadn't acted quickly enough. The last time, her little scheme had actually gotten off the ground. From the moment she made her Yuletide vow, it had been an endless barrage of her company.

She'd shown up with coffee, shown up with whiskey and flowers. She'd tagged along with him and Gabriel when they went jogging. She'd gotten a membership to his gym.

He'd been so close to killing her. So very close.

I have that power, now. I could send Jules away on assignment, and—

"You know what," she interrupted, "right now...I bet you're plotting against me." She snapped her fingers with a beaming smile. "See, we have that in common! We both like to plot!"

He let out a sigh, feeling abruptly tired. "Why are you doing this? It's genuinely the worst of our games."

"It's not a game," she said frankly. "I care about you. And not just because of Julian. I care about *you*, Devon. As a *person*." She rested a hand on his chest. "In here."

He stood there blankly, then blinked three times in rapid succession.

"What are you doing?" she asked.

"I'm making sure I'm not frozen."

She took a step closer, beaming all the while. "You're not frozen. You're starting to thaw."

He stepped back just as far, reaching for his Taser. "It's never going to work."

She considered a moment, then flashed a pearly smile. "It worked on Julian."

Julian's always been weak.

"Good luck finding coffee, the cafeteria's all out." She headed inside, tossing a look over her shoulder. "And be careful with that—the safety mechanism's a little fidgety."

Fidgety?

He stared down at it, utterly frozen. "This is just...a perfect metaphor for my whole day."

Chapter 4

Gabriel paced back into his office, swinging the door shut. It had been a long night, and the day wasn't turning out to be any better. No sooner had he gotten into his car and dragged himself to Guilder, than half the PC agents training in the Oratory decided to storm the neighborhood monastery—waving fists and pointed sticks.

Devon had handled it well, he could admit that. When they raised their voices and started shouting, he got quiet instead. Sincere. Demanding. It was a strange combination of the fox's own making—one he had mastered over the years, one he used without hesitation on friends and foes alike. *You must do this, because you are worthy of it. You must not do that, it is beneath you.*

A clever twist of logic, one that rarely failed to get results. Today, it might have averted a supernatural uprising in the English countryside. But Gabriel had given him no credit. Gabriel had barely been able to speak. His people were angry? Well, he was angry with them—for being so stupid about it. He didn't want to waste his time explaining things they should already know.

But you should. That's what a president does.

He sank into his chair with a sigh, roasting in the heat of the newly-discovered fireplace. A part of him was tempted to turn it off, but he was too taken with the novelty. He slumped onto the desk instead, resting his cheek on the cool wood and staring without blinking at the twisting flames.

They danced before his eyes as a familiar voice rang through his head.

"It's going to be an exciting morning, Gabriel. Are you ready for it?"
Knock, knock.
He lifted his head, just as the door opened and a cloud of ivory hair sailed inside. His first reaction was utter shock—she wasn't meant to return for ages. Yet, he was thoroughly unsurprised.
I called for a bedtime story. Of course she came home.
"I hope you scheduled an appointment," he said by means of a greeting. "My time is quite valuable these days, and the hours are rarely my own."
Angel glanced between him and the fireplace, vaguely surprised to see it in use. "Yes, I can see you're very busy."
Without another word, she flung her bag onto one of the recliners and started the slow process of disarming herself. A blade from each shoe, another from each leg. Another from each wrist. Guns in both holsters. A strange metallic device that looked distressingly like a crab.
When she was finished, she plopped into the chair next to his. "I ran into Devon outside," she announced brightly, spinning around in a circle.
Gabriel rolled his eyes, *thrilled beyond words* she was there. "Oh yeah, what was he doing?"
She shrugged. "Cradling explosives, and feeling sorry for himself."
The usual.
"You must help me destroy him," he commanded.
"Can't do it, brosef," she replied cheerfully, giving the chair another spin. "I have my own campaign against him—I can't do anything but smile."
"I'm asking for a favor—"
"And when was the last time you did *me* a favor?" she countered.
"I'm serious, Gabriel. I've got this whole thing going on. I can't quit in the middle just because you don't like the guy."
He pursed his lips, growing suddenly stern. "What did we decide on the mountain?"

Her face went still. "I don't want to talk about it," she muttered.

"What did we decide on the mountain, Angela?"

There was a reluctant pause.

"We decided on pain of death to aid in each other's vendettas," she recited wearily.

He nodded soundly, never breaking that exacting gaze. "And if our vendettas interfered?"

"Then as the oldest sibling, you were given broad discretionary powers to decide what was best." She flashed a childish scowl. "You know, I never liked that part. You can't hold me to that."

"Yes, I can."

"I was *six*, Gabriel!" she exclaimed, spinning even faster. "There's an argument to be made that you shouldn't have dragged me to the top of that particular mountain in the first place."

He flicked his fingers, bringing the chair to a sudden halt. "Well *that's* where they built the altar, so *that's* where we had to go," he said decisively, as if that settled the matter. "Besides, I didn't drag you. You were bloody eager."

"You told me it was a prison for mice. You said we were going to set them all free—"

"I don't want to talk about it," he interrupted moodily, shuffling the papers on his desk. He stapled a few of them, just having to do something with his hands, then let out a strained breath and removed them again with his ink. "Why are you here? I thought you had another few days."

"I did have another few days," she said calmly, rummaging in Devon's side of the desk. He had locked the drawers, but she pulled a pin from her hair and started working. "But then I got a call from my big brother and decided to speed things up." Those sapphire eyes flashed up, assessing him intently. "How much sleep did you get last night? Did you go out walking after our call?"

Gabriel turned his face, unwilling to answer.

He had gone out walking, but he didn't want to talk about it. The longer they sat there, the more he realized he didn't want to talk about anything at all.

Instead of answering, he pushed to his feet, abruptly claustrophobic. "You want to spar?"

She lifted her eyebrows in surprise. "Right now?"

"Yeah"—he turned off the fireplace—"why not?"

THERE WAS A SELDOM viewed plaque in the corner of the locker room—a calendar, of sorts, to commemorate every special occasion that had happened on Guilder soil.

It had been put up so long ago, nearly every box was filled. There were all the predictable dates: holidays, defections, graduations, rebellions. Then there were the days specific to the Oratory itself. The day it had caught fire in a twisted time loop. The day, not long before, when a blue-eyed teenager had transformed it into a swamp. There was the time that Victor Mallins had assumed the sole presidency, the night that Rae Kerrigan had been the first inmate to break out of jail.

But on the seventeenth of October, there was different kind of mark. A tiny star had been placed in the corner to commemorate the first time that Cromfield's two retired lieutenants had signed their employment contracts, walked into the Oratory, and started to spar.

It had been marked for two reasons: because of the impact on the building, and because of the impact on every man and woman inside. Today was looking to be more of the same.

"Is that a trident?"

Gabriel stopped in the middle of the mats as his sister pulled out a gleaming silver pole and started twisting at the edges. Sure enough, three shining prongs appeared at the end. The rest of it lengthened and sharpened and lengthened again, until the slim baton it had come from was nothing more than a memory, and a weapon that was as fearsome as it was majestic appeared in its place.

She gave it a cursory twirl, flashing a breathless grin. "Gabriel, it's telescopic. See?" She twisted it proudly back and forth, demonstrating how easy it would be to slide into her coat. "At this point, it's just practical."

The assassin nodded slowly. "Yes, it is."

I must have one.

"Well, I don't care about any of that," he said carelessly, throwing a jealous look over his shoulder, "you and your mermaid weapons. But if you happened to have a spare—"

She pulled out another, tossing it into his hand.

Bloody hell!

He caught it without thinking, examining the quality from handle to point with something close to reverence. A full minute passed before he finally looked into his sister's eyes.

"I love you very much. Have I told you that lately?"

She snorted with laughter. "Let's see if you still love me, after I kick your arse."

With an involuntary grin, he followed her to the very center of the chamber, oblivious to the way the rest of the agents scattered as they walked past. Most days, the presence of even one of the siblings would have been enough to warrant an immediate exodus—for safety reasons, if nothing else—but they'd seen the tridents. It was impossible to leave a situation involving tridents.

A few of them had already started recording on their phones.

"Have you ever fought with one of these before?" Angel called, falling into position. Her shoes were gone, and her ivory hair and been woven back into a practical braid.

Not recently. Not on land.

"Of course," Gabriel replied without thinking, flicking the end of a prong. It sounded with an immensely satisfying *ting*, and a little smile crept up his face. "I was born for this."

She planted hers on the mats, standing beside it like a god of the sea. "Show me."

From that point on, there was very little speaking. It took breath to speak, and those breaths were needed someplace else. In the blink of an eye, the room and everything in it disappeared; it was just the two of them again. Circling and crossing, prodding and testing, freezing in moments of unnatural stillness, before flying towards each other with the brimming vibrance of two young gods.

The tridents sang as they kissed each other, before scraping themselves apart—each new revolution like the circling of stars that had caught in each other's orbits. There was only so long they could keep distance before those forces would send them colliding again.

One would strike, and the other would parry. One would launch themselves high into the air, and the other would somersault beneath their feet. It was a dance they were doing. It was shock and flash, bruised fingers and streaks of lightning. But beneath it all—the dodging and panting, the lunging and striking—there lay a great discipline. An invisible tether, grounding them to the earth.

"Come on," she taunted, keeping out of reach, "is that all you've got?"

He lifted his eyes with a bloody grin, spinning the trident above his head.

It had taken only a few minutes to accustom himself to the grip. A few minutes after that, he was already taking chances. It didn't help that he'd been mainlining caffeine since around two in the morning, or that the gleaming metal was sparking his tatù to life.

Instead of answering his sister directly, he sprinted suddenly forward and then vaulted into the air—spinning the trident above him like a propeller. Higher and higher it lifted him, until the tip of his golden hair brushed against the domed ceiling. There was a gasp from their invisible audience, Angel lifted her head—wary and impatient. Then when he was ready, only when he was ready, he fixed his eyes on the point of impact and flew like an arrow back down to earth.

"Gabriel!"

A voice called out just as he landed, stealing a fraction of concentration and sending him rolling over the floor. He managed to take Angel with him, that was the best he could say. He even managed to knock her around a little, but at that point, they were both laughing so hard, it was impossible to say who had won. Probably neither of them, probably both. On the other side of the Oratory, an agent slipped into the locker room, adding another tiny star to the plaque on the wall.

"You see what I mean?" Angel panted, untangling her braid from a silver prong. "It's just practical." She hoisted onto her elbows, peering towards the door. "Who just called you?"

Gabriel looked over at the same time to see Dash and Rob by the door. They were bruised and battered, but grinning. They had brought a briefcase—one that took both of them to carry.

He stared at the case, his smile already fading. "Can you get Devon?" he asked quietly.

But the fox was already there. He'd seen the pair walking across the grass from the cafeteria and appeared only a moment after, just in time to see Gabriel dive like a comet into the floor.

"If you're done playing Little Mermaid, we've got some business, Alden."

Angel lifted her eyebrows, while the assassin tightened his grip.

I could stab him. He eyed the gleaming prongs. *I could stab him three times.*

"Coming, dearest!"

JUST A FEW MINUTES later, Gabriel was stepped back into his office, holding open the door for the three men who filed in just behind. He hadn't been expecting Rob and Dash to come back so quickly. Theirs had been one of the toughest assignments, so he was glad they'd come back at all.

"So what's this?" Devon asked immediately, gesturing to the briefcase. He'd been similarly thrilled to see them, but his curiosity had been piqued. "Why are you holding it like that?"

Dash merely flashed a boyish grin, while Rob reached into his bag.

"Not so fast...this is for you," Rob said. The eagle pulled out a bright swath of fabric, tossing it across the room. It unfurled halfway there, cascading open to reveal the folds of a full-length dress.

...not what I was expecting.

"For me?" Devon caught it automatically, staring in confusion. "What—"

"You said if I took a friend to Aleppo, you'd wear whatever I wanted," Rob answered, gesturing to the gown. "I think this will bring me joy."

For a moment, all of them stared at each other.

Then all of them stared at the dress.

It looked like the kind of thing a person might wear to Carnival, or some other fantastical spectacle. It looked like the kind of thing that had come with a feathered headdress and rhinestones, but over the course of a trans-continental flight, most of those things had started to fall off. As if that wasn't enough, there was the color—a vibrant yellow hue, that was almost painful to look at straight on. Of course, the designers had found a way around this by cutting out so many geometric pieces of fabric, it was clear that whatever the celebration, it wasn't meant to be worn very long.

Gabriel stared in silence, aching for a camera.

This is SO much better than the swimsuit.

"Alright," Devon played along, fighting back a smile. He rolled up the gown with one hand, gesturing to the briefcase with another. "Now, what did you guys find?"

Dash tilted his head curiously, whispering in the eagle's ear. "Does he not understand what to do with it?"

"You're meant to *wear* it, Devon." Rob gestured once more with a beaming smile, looking happier than his friends had seen him years. "As we agreed."

The office went quiet for a moment. Then Devon sighed and began taking off his shirt.

"The briefcase," he demanded, reaching for the dress. "Before I take my own life."

Seriously, best day ever.

The men shared a conspiratorial grin, then heaved the case onto the desk—laying it carefully on its side. There was a quiet *creak* as Rob unlatched the hinges, pulling it open in a grand reveal.

Gabriel took a step closer, the smile freezing on his face.

"It's some kind of new metal," Dash said authoritatively. "We're not sure what it's called, but it was the only thing of value left in the munition's yard, and when we spoke to the man in charge of security, he said a person had come just that morning and tried to take it away."

Devon paced to the desk in complete astonishment, the yellow fabric swishing around his feet. "It's called tambor," he replied, flashing a look at Gabriel. "We just found some ourselves." He shook his head, trying to make sense of it. "They *tried* to take it away?"

"It was too heavy," Rob replied simply. "It took the two of us just to get it onto a truck."

It was quiet for a moment, then Dash cleared his throat.

"So what is it?" he asked. "What does this mean?"

Devon cast another look at Gabriel.

"It means, you did good," he said reassuringly. "And together," he added, with the hint of a smile. "If things went so well, maybe we should pair up the two of you more often."

The shifters exchanged a swift glance before flashing the same wicked smile.

"Did you hear that?" Dash asked innocently. "*Really* subtle, that was."

Rob pursed his lips, like the whole thing was adorable. "Just look at him, playing matchmaker in his little dress."

The fox himself snorted with laughter, battling the tight fabric, as he waved them both to the door. "Alright, you've had your fun. Go drink it off somewhere. Speak of this to no one."

That seems unlikely.

The two friends waited until the shifters had left—listening as they made their way loudly down the hall—before turning to each other. They stared a moment, then turned back to the case.

"What are the odds Kraigan was using the same stuff?" Devon asked quietly.

Gabriel shook his head, unwilling to consider the answer. "I don't know, but they didn't get what they were after. That means—"

"That means, they'll be looking for more," Devon finished, mind racing a hundred miles a minute as he tried to figure out their next steps. "But that doesn't really help us. Luke said this stuff was as rare as it got. If they didn't get it in Aleppo, I don't know where they might—"

"I know where there's more," Gabriel interrupted softly.

The fox stared in astonishment. "You do?"

The assassin let out a quiet sigh. "Yeah, I do."

The two men packed up their belongings and headed out of the office. There were plans to make and stories to share, but they would do it somewhere brighter, somewhere above ground.

"You guys heading out?" Haley called, as they opened the door. "I could find a…" She trailed off, staring in bewilderment.

It took Gabriel a second to realize what had caught her attention. At the same time, he heard the jingle of tiny bells. He pointed to the hem of Devon's dress. "Those are festive."

The fox let out a strangled gasp, having already forgotten.

"Are we going to talk about this?" Haley asked curiously.

There was a beat of silence, then Devon streaked back into the office.

I guess not.

Chapter 5

Devon woke at the crack of dawn, blinking slowly at the ceiling.
It was the most sleep he'd gotten in longer than he could remember—almost five whole hours—but it hadn't prepared him in the slightest for whatever madness the day might bring.

Despite the pressing urgency of the situation, Gabriel hadn't been very forthcoming about his history with the strange metal. Nor had he volunteered any ideas about why it had popped up on their radar twice in just a few days. He had been very clear, however, about what needed to happen next. They were venturing into his old world, the shadowy underbelly of London where he and Angel had cut their teeth. In order to do so, the fox would need to follow a specific set of rules.

His instructions had been simple, yet utterly strange. He must wear a dark coat, with a hoodie. He must bring a pack of cigarettes and a lighter. He must not shower. He must not shave.

Maybe there's an actual reason for it. Maybe he found us new jobs at the circus.

With a little sigh, Devon swung his feet to the floor—stretching his arms, as he stared at the slate grey sky behind the curtains. He showered anyway, but panicked and got out halfway through, trailing wisps of sweetly-scented steam, as he padded back into the bedroom.

Rae was still sleeping in the center of the bed, one arm flung across her face, as the other had wedged itself somehow behind the headboard. He coaxed it free with a little smile, perching on the blankets beside her. When he'd gotten home the night before, he'd recited Gabriel's instructions and asked for her counsel—but she'd merely inquired if the yellow gown sticking out of his bag had something to do with the swimsuit he'd brought back from Texas. Then she'd asked if there was *anything important he'd like to tell her*. He'd stopped speaking to her after that, and climbed into bed.

"Rae," he whispered, giving her a delicate shake, "open your eyes."

She sank defiantly deeper into the bed, reaching blindly for his throat, but he caught her wrist with another smile—shaking her again, as he kissed the tips of her fingers.

"Honey, I need a quick favor."

She flipped onto her side, mumbling into the pillow. "What favor?"

"Could you conjure me a pack of cigarettes?"

One eye peeled open, then another. She blinked at him a moment, wondering if she'd misheard, then she shook her head with an ominous expression—twirling her magical fingers. "This job is really changing you, Devon."

He flashed a grin, stuffing it into his pocket. "Thanks, love."

She fell immediately back to sleep as he jogged downstairs—turning on various lights as he went. There hadn't been a specific time they were meeting, the assassin had merely instructed him to be ready at dawn. Devon had nodded, straight-faced, and asked if they'd be dueling with pistols or sabers. He'd thought this was hilarious. Gabriel hadn't cracked a smile.

No sense of humor, that guy.

He grabbed a water bottle from the fridge, wondering if there was time to make something for breakfast, then turned in surprise as the sound of light footsteps headed up the front walk.

By the time he opened the door, Gabriel was already standing on the porch.

"Morning," he said shortly, giving the fox a quick assessment. He nodded at the choice of clothes, before stepping closer with a sudden frown. "Did you shower?"

Devon inched backwards with a flush. "No," he said guiltily. "Did you just smell me?"

The assassin turned on his heel. "Get in the car."

After sending up a quick prayer, Devon stuffed the water back into the fridge and followed the assassin outside—only to come to an immediate stop on the sidewalk. There was indeed a car parked in front of his house, but it wasn't anything he recognized. It wasn't anything built within the last century. To be honest, it was hard to identify as a car, beneath the layers of soot and dirt.

"Nice ride," he said tentatively, hovering on the sidewalk. There was a judgmental twitch of curtains from a house across the street. "Where did it come from?"

"I got it last night," Gabriel said impatiently, getting into the driver's seat. "Get inside, Devon, we're going to be late."

The fox opened the passenger door, sliding obediently onto the cracked leather. He must be perfectly compliant, or he'd get left behind. He'd been forced to swear an oath the night before.

This is...cozy.

For whatever reason, he'd expected the car to be clean on the inside—a perfect camouflage to gain them entry wherever they were meant to go. But the thing was a mess: cracked dashboard, smeared windows, a sea of empty take-out containers and candy wrappers littered across the floor.

His eyes fell upon a pair of crumbled receipts, both bearing the same name.

"You got this last night," he quoted, glancing at Gabriel. "Does that mean you stole it?"

The assassin slipped a metal rod into the ignition. "Hmm?"

"Is this somebody's car?" Devon repeated a bit louder, grinding his teeth in frustration.

Before the assassin could answer, he reached for the glove-box—hoping to find a name on the registration. It slammed shut before he could touch it, the locking mechanism sealing over.

"Hands to yourself," Gabriel instructed. "It's another of your rules."

Devon rolled his eyes, wondering what he'd gotten himself into. "You and your rules," he muttered. "Half the time, I think you just made them up. Were you fighting with a trident yesterday?" he added suddenly, remembering his friend's mythological spiral from the ceiling. "Where did you get one? How did you even learn to fight with one?"

I know you didn't grow up watching Disney films.

Gabriel brightened with a true smile.

"It functions essentially the same as a spatula," he explained, mimicking the gesture. "And that was the last of them, I'm afraid. You'll have to stick with regular spears."

"The last one, huh?" Devon quipped. "In the whole world?"

"That's right."

There was a pause.

"Just drive the car, Alden."

The assassin flashed a wicked smile, throwing it into gear. "Buckle up."

***

IT WAS A STRANGE FEELING, flying across the city whilst having no idea where he was going. But given the man sitting beside him, Devon had learned to accept a certain level of strange. Instead of asking questions that were sure to get shot down, he fished out his phone—fingers flying across the keys as he typed out a quick message.

"What's that?" Gabriel asked, glancing over disapprovingly. "I'm pretty sure I said *no phones*, Devon. I'm pretty sure that was one of your rules."

"It wasn't," the fox answered distractedly, pressing *send*. "I checked."

"You checked," the assassin repeated under his breath, fingers drumming restlessly on the steering wheel. "Who are you texting anyway? Who would possibly be awake at this hour?"

Don't tell him. He'll only tease you.

Devon bit his lip.

If you DON'T tell him, he'll steal your phone.

"I'm keeping Julian appraised of how it's going," he answered casually, as if it scarcely mattered. "Given the nature of our business, he advised me not to go to a second location."

Gabriel laughed in spite of himself, raking back a tangle of hair. "You said the same thing the first time I asked you to go drinking."

"And I was right, wasn't I?" Devon countered, flashing him a hard look. "You'd arranged for a photographer to take some 'tasteful pictures,' the second I was too drunk to say no."

The assassin nodded sagely. "There's a lesson to be learned there."

"I should find better friends?"

"You should be nicer to the ones you already have," Gabriel answered, making a hairpin turn at a streetlight. "Otherwise, they might feel the need to be memorable."

Memorable.

Devon snorted with laughter.

That's one way of looking at it.

They turned on the radio and drove about twenty more minutes, flying across the familiar streets, and towards the industrial district on the other side of town. The fox stared out the window as the houses got smaller and smaller, as the businesses were shuttered or run-down, before the assassin made a sudden turn and angled them down towards the river.

He typed another quick message to Julian, straightening up in alarm.

"Are we going to the docks?" he asked, as the distant water loomed into view. "I swear, Gabriel, if you dragged me all the way out here to look at your boat—"

The car veered abruptly off the road, screeching to a stop along the curb.

Devon let out a gasp, throwing out both hands to catch himself. Even with his advanced reflexes, he nearly concussed himself on the crooked dash. But when he threw a wild look to the other side of the car, the assassin was calm as ever. They had merely arrived at their destination.

"What the—"

"The metal I saw is located in an old safe house of Cromfield's," Gabriel said unexpectedly, easing the car a few feet forward so they were in clear view of the docks. "Unfortunately, the address of the safe house is a little hard to come by—but this is a good first step."

Devon stared at him in amazement, then made a concerted effort to close his mouth. "...okay."

"Now, I don't want to frighten you, Wardell," the assassin continued, "but there are illegal gambling rings scattered throughout every major city in the world." He lowered his voice to a conspiratorial whisper, tilting their heads together. "Even our dear London."

The fox gritted his teeth, striving for patience. "You don't say."

"The person we're looking for is undoubtedly at one of these rings," Gabriel continued, "but in order to avoid interference from people like you, the locations change each morning."

There was a fleeting pause.

"People like *us*," Devon corrected, with a pointed look. "In order to avoid interference from people like *us*—the locations change each morning."

The assassin flashed a banal smile. "Sure."

Heaven help me.

"Alright," the fox said briskly, "so who decides where these rings move?"

"Now *that's* an interesting question..." Gabriel replied, leaning back in his chair. The man might have had two millions pounds of Italian chrome parked in his driveway, but he looked just as at home sitting in a dilapidated clunker he'd found behind the local pawnshop. "Originally, it was tasked to just one person—but when he got picked up in Manila for solicitation—it was decided that a rotating circle of people would decide. I was on that circle myself once," he added with a touch of pride. He flushed defensively when Devon raised his eyebrows. "They don't ask just anyone. Of course, I had to decline," he concluded sadly. "A bunch of people went drag-racing through the Gobi Desert for solstice, and I'd already promised Angel we could go. I kept the letter, though."

A sudden quiet fell over the car, as both men stared through opposite windows.

"I'll never understand your life," Devon said faintly.

"Come on." Gabriel clapped him on the shoulder, yanking open the door. "You're about to see it firsthand."

On that ominous note, they left the car on the side of the road—pulling up their hoods and cramming their hands into pockets, as they made their way against a strong headwind towards the distant pier. The gusts were even stronger coming off the water, suffused with that icy winter mist that sees clothing as a challenge and seeps right into your bones. For a split second, Devon was unable to see anything past it. He bowed his head to escape the worst of it, shivering in his coat.

"Bloody hell, it's cold," he muttered.

Gabriel led him around a corner, then came to a sudden stop. "Hence, the grates."

The fox lifted his head in astonishment to see the entire city of London wasn't sleeping after all. Around twenty people were gathered in tight clusters around the industrial heating vents that lined the waterfront—sipping bitingly hot coffee, as they warmed their hands over the steam. Each of them had the same red nose, calloused hands, and chapped eyebrows. Each of them was wearing the same nondescript hoodie. Each of them was sporting the same scruff.

Devon glanced down at his clothes, catching the faint whiff of shampoo.

He's right, I shouldn't have showered.

"Morning, boys!" Gabriel strolled right down the center of the pier, waving to a few familiar faces, before selecting a grate for himself. "You still have all your fingers?"

The fox trailed after him, keeping his eyes on the ground.

"Barely," an older man grunted in reply. "I've never seen a winter so cold." As if to echo the sentiment, the winds thrashed even harder. "You wouldn't happen to have a cigarette, would you?"

Without thinking, Devon reached into his pocket—holding out a pack. The man glanced at him in surprise, then took one gratefully, placing it with trembling fingers between his lips.

"Much obliged," he said, leaning forward as the fox pulled out a lighter. "Haven't seen you around these parts before. You just come in on a trawler?"

"We've been working out of Brighton," Gabriel answered without missing a beat. "Good work if you can get it, but they've got more hands than they need. You between shipments?"

The man nodded, blowing out smoke. "When am I not?"

The three of them chuckled quietly, then returned to the grate.

Never in his life, had Devon seen a stranger assortment of people. It reminded him of those deep sea vents—the briny crustaceans that would huddle around them, looking for warmth. A labor strike had been in the cards for months. He'd spoken with Philip about it the last time they sparred.

"You got here late," the old man said suddenly, glancing towards the thick metal sheeting on the buildings that lined the pier. "When that foreman opens the door, there's going to be about two dozen people in line ahead of you. Shouldn't have slept in so late."

"Nah, my car wouldn't start." Gabriel gestured to the wreck across the street. "Then I had to wait for this princess to wake up," he teased, giving Devon a playful shove. "Anyways, we just got paid—figured we'd try to pick up an extra shift to keep the women happy."

The man let out a bark of laughter, nodding along. "They like us better out of the house, don't they?"

"They certainly do." Gabriel backed a step away, squinting against the wind. "Well if you've already got enough to fill a shift, I guess we'll start looking for somewhere to lose our paychecks." He patted his jacket with a mischievous grin. "You wouldn't happen to know where the game is today, would you?"

"Ponies or poker?"

"Poker."

The man scratched his chin, thinking it over. His eyes found all those careful little details, lingering on the broken car. "It's down at Coventry Hall," he concluded. "Password's magpie."

"Thanks, mate." Gabriel clapped him on the back, glancing up as one of those metal doors slid open. "Looks like you can finally get out of the wind."

"Good riddance." The man chuckled, and ambled away.

Devon kept pace with the assassin as they wove through the throng of people, feeling like he'd drifted into a different word. His skin was screaming from the icy gusts of wind blowing off the water, and his head was spinning with things he didn't understand.

Coventry Hall. Magpie.

He had assumed that Gabriel was being hyperbolic. Or more likely, the assassin was using the opportunity to have himself a little fun. But there was truth in everything he'd said, a reason for each of his nonsensical rules. How was it possible that such a thing existed—a thriving culture in the heart of the city? A secret society layered invisibly atop his own?

"This way."

He followed along as Gabriel led him away from the street where they'd parked, and to a semi-vacant lot on the other side of the buildings. The assassin paused a moment at the chain-link fence, then moved with sudden purpose—leaping over the top and landing lightly on the other side.

"So wait a second, we're all good?" Devon asked, trailing haplessly behind him. "Everything that guy said: Coventry Hall, magpie...you know what that means?"

Gabriel smiled a little, never slowing his pace. "I know what that means."

"And are you going to tell me?" the fox pressed with irritation, quickening his stride. Of all the many things that bothered him about the assassin, there was nothing worse than that maddening smile. "This person we're looking for—you never even told me their name."

"Didn't I?"

Gabriel came to a sudden stop, gazing around the parking lot. Without thinking, Devon came to a stop beside him—still fuming, still spinning, so completely out of sorts, that he didn't immediately recognize the appraising expression on the assassin's face.

"What are you doing?" he finally prompted.

"Browsing," Gabriel replied.

Devon nodded absentmindedly before it suddenly clicked. "Wait—what?"

He made a wild grab to stop him, but the assassin was already moving—sweeping across the frosted pavement towards a specific car at the edge of the lot. He wasted no time once he was there; he merely rifled in his pocket—as though searching for keys—then waved his fingers over the door.

The locks popped up and he slipped inside, motioning for Devon to do the same. "Get in."

"Absolutely not!" Devon protested, looking wildly for cameras. "Whose car is this?!"

"I don't know."

"Gabriel!"

The assassin let out a frustrated breath, then rifled around in the glove compartment, yanking out a paper and reading it in the pale light. "Harry Atkins, an electronics specialist from Kent. Now get inside."

"Stop it," Devon hissed, resisting the urge to drag him out by the hair. "We can't just steal this guy's car, Gabriel. Are you trying to get us arrested?"

"We can't just show up to an illegal gambling ring in a registered vehicle," Gabriel countered without expression. "Are you trying to get us *killed*?"

They stared at each other in seething silence, then Devon got into the car.

Each movement was blunt and efficient. He refused to meet the assassin's gaze. When at last the silence became too much, he lifted his chin—speaking in clenched teeth to the road.

"I'm returning this as soon as we're finished."

Gabriel hid a smile, tapping a finger to the ignition. "I'd expect nothing less."

THE CO-PRESIDENTS PULLED out of the parking lot without incident, without sirens, and eased back onto the city roads. Before five minutes had passed, they were just another car in a sea of endless commuters. Only a few minutes after that, Gabriel rolled to a stop beside a bakery.

He ordered two coffees and a raspberry strudel. Then they were back on the road.

The miles dragged past as they inched through the morning traffic. Gabriel downed his coffee in the first minute, but the fox had yet to touch his own. His arms were folded tightly and he was staring out the window—refusing to acknowledge the man driving the car.

"What," Gabriel finally asked, "are you not speaking to me now?" He tried and failed to catch the fox's gaze. "You're really going to side with Harry Atkins, electronics specialist, over me?"

I would side with ANYONE over you.

Devon turned to face him, twisting in his chair. "At any point, were you planning on telling the council about this gambling ring? At any point, did you consider maybe *not* stealing some guy's car? Requesting an unregistered one instead?"

Gabriel stiffened and reached for the radio. "I liked you better quiet—"

Devon slapped his hand down. "You get that we have rules for a reason, right?" he asked sharply. "You get that we shut down gambling rings for a reason? That we do these things, for a *reason*?"

The assassin met his gaze, then flashed that same infuriating smile. "Sure."

Forget it.

Devon let out a hard breath, turning back to the window. His fingers drummed restlessly on his phone, while his eyes passed over the scenery with a distracted frown.

A full minute passed before Gabriel threw him a sideways look.

"Her name is Mary."

The fox glanced over in surprise. "What?"

"The person we're looking for—her name is Mary."

They pulled over before Devon could answer, rolling to a stop alongside a brick building he must have passed a thousand times before. He glanced up at the letterhead, trying to place it, but either by intention or a quirk of English weather, the name was faded beyond recognition.

Coventry Hall.

"I'll just be a minute," Gabriel said, unbuckling his seatbelt. "You should stay in the car."

Devon froze in surprise, halfway out the door himself. "What are you talking about?"

"Those were dockworkers," the assassin replied, pointing back the way they'd come, "hard-working men trying to blow off a little steam. The guys in here—they're actual criminals."

The fox raised a sarcastic eyebrow. "You're saying it might be dangerous?"

"I'm saying some of them might know you."

...oh.

Devon considered a moment, then shook his head.

"So they know me," he said dismissively, getting out of the car, "who cares. If they really know me, they'll scatter. We need something in that building. I'm not staying the bloomin' stolen car."

The assassin regarded him with a peculiar expression, then nodded. "Alright."

"Alright?" Devon quoted bitingly, joining him on the sidewalk. "That's it? You're not going to tell me I'm being an idiot, and melt the locks into the door?"

Gabriel shook his head with a faint smile, striding towards the building. "Not at all. You said it yourself—if they know you, they'll scatter. Or they might try to shoot you," he added thoughtfully. "Depends on how much they've had to drink, I guess." He stopped at the door, knocking a rhythmic pattern.

It swung open a second later.

"Magpie," he said without hesitation.

It opened a bit further, and the two of them slipped inside.

Whatever image Devon might have conjured of an illegal gambling ring, it was exceeded at every turn. If he hadn't known it was a regular weekday morning, he might have thought they had wandered through the doors at the moment of some great celebration. A championship win, or a beloved holiday. Something to explain the brimming energy that seemed to rattle in the air.

There were five round tables set at the various corners, with one in the center. An ever-rotating cast of people wandered in between. They were loud and vibrant, crackling with laughter and mostly drunk. It was barely eleven in the morning, but already, he could smell the fumes rising from their skin. A host of nameless waiters flitted amongst them, serving whiskey and gin.

Gabriel caught one of them as he hurried past. "I'm looking for Mary."

It seemed like a longshot, but the man pointed without hesitation. The assassin thanked him, and together, he and Devon made their way slowly across the floor.

It was the kind of place that made one want to linger, the kind of place he might have enjoyed with Julian—a rowdy corner of the city to decompress after a long mission. The poker itself was more of an afterthought, although those jubilant voices occasionally erupted into shouts. If the games were fixed, Devon wasn't able to see how. Not at a glance, maybe not ever.

Maybe they have ink, he thought suddenly. *Maybe that's how they're doing it.*

He lingered in Gabriel's shadow as they pushed their way through the crowd, watching with amusement as people started to recognize him, one after another. One man let out a cry of delight upon seeing him—calling him Rafael and kissing both cheeks. Another woman saw him coming and flashed a preemptive scowl, pulling a fifty-pound note from her pocket and slapping it into his hand.

Still another man they never even noticed. He'd been sitting in the shadows, and slipped out the back the second they arrived. The last time they'd seen each other, he'd inadvertently exploded a dumpster.

The time before that, it had been an ice cream parlor. He wouldn't linger for a third.

"So who's this Mary?" Devon asked once they'd cleared the tables and got to somewhere a little quieter. The rooms narrowed into corridors, which eventually lifted into stairs.

"Mary DeWinter is a chemist," Gabriel replied, his ears still ringing from the din in the next room. "She's also the only person alive who knows the address of the safe house."

Devon followed behind him, stair after stair. "Mary DeWinter," he repeated flatly. "Are you telling me that's her real name?"

The assassin snorted with laughter. "No, it's not," he admitted. "But for the purposes of our exercise, Mary DeWinter is a chemist that will be able to brew us exactly what we need." He glanced up a bit nervously, as they reached the top stairs. "If she remembers me..."

They paused a moment on the landing, gathering themselves together, before Gabriel drew in a deep breath and knocked upon the door. It was quiet a few seconds, then he knocked again.

Please, let her be here. Please, let her remember.

There was a sound from somewhere further inside the room, soft footsteps shuffling toward the door. A second later, it creaked open and a tiny old woman appeared in the frame.

She was smaller than anyone Devon had ever seen in real life. So small, he felt the need to move in permanently and protect her. Her bones were bent and her shoulders were drooping. Her face was lined with so many creases and wrinkles, it looked as though she'd been left out in the sun.

Only her eyes remained untouched. Bright and brown and brimming with secrets.

They fell upon Gabriel and sparked with the purest joy. "Oh, sweetheart!"

The assassin stepped forward with a tender smile and embraced her, bending so low that his knees nearly scraped the floor. They stayed like that for a long time—swaying ever so slightly, her bony arms wrapped around his neck—before finally pulling apart.

"I've missed you," she murmured, fingertips pressing to her lips. Her eyes swept him up and down, soaking in the details. "It's been so long, Gabriel. I wasn't sure I'd ever see you again."

"Nonsense," he replied, reaching into his jacket with a grin. "You think I could stay away?"

She burst out laughing when he presented the strudel—such a quintessential grandmotherly laugh, Devon couldn't help but smile himself. Despite her age and creaking bones, she reached forward with eager hands, popping open the lid and taking a great sniff.

"My favorite—you remembered!" Her bright eyes travelled a bit further, resting on the dark-haired man by his side. "And who's this? I don't think you've ever brought anyone besides Angie."

Devon glanced over with a touch of surprise as Gabriel gestured between them.

"There's a reason for that. This is a good friend of mine." He took a step closer, lowering his voice. "Mary, I need to find something I left with you. An address...I'm hoping you still have it."

"Of course I still have it," she answered without pause. "I've kept everything you've ever given me." She studied him closely, reading the lines of his face. "But are you sure?"

He hesitated for a split second, then nodded.

"Alright, then. Wait here."

Without another word, she vanished into the apartment—returning only a moment later with a tiny slip of paper that she pressed into his hand. Their heads bent low together, and she whispered something into his ear, giving him an affectionate pat on the cheek. He rolled his eyes and kissed her in return, already backing away towards the stairs.

"Say goodbye, Devon."

The fox opened his mouth in surprise, but the door was already swinging shut. The last thing he saw was a flash of the woman's bright eyes as she offered him a parting smile.

He smiled in return, then she was gone.

"That's it?" he asked in surprise, turning towards his friend. Gabriel was already halfway down the stairs, beckoning him impatiently. "What did she say to you? There at the end?"

The assassin flashed a look over his shoulder. "She said you look like a narc."

Liar.

Devon jogged after him with a little grin, peeling back the layers one after another. He'd written off the criminal underworld as a shadow realm full of bad people, doing bad things. They had been taught to think as much at Guilder. But there were layers to it he'd never understood until that moment. And whatever way you spliced it, there was nothing bad about that woman. She was probably in her kitchen—delightfully choking down pieces of raspberry strudel.

"So you've never brought anyone else, huh?" He caught up with Gabriel, wrapping an arm around his shoulder with a broad smile. "Only me—your good friend?"

"The man who insisted on coming?" the assassin corrected, trying to shake him loose. "I've also brought Angel. We've gone together a dozen times before."

"I never count Angel," Devon replied, tightening his grip. "And in the future, I'd prefer if we come here together. It can be our special place. Just me and my good friend."

<hr>

BACK IN THE CAR, THERE was a significantly lighter mood than before. Instead of brooding in silence, the men turned on the radio and even started singing along—miming the electric guitar and drum riffs and every stoplight. They found a drive-thru and got more coffee. The sun broke through the clouds. By the time they crossed through downtown and started winding their way back to their little corner of London, it was actually shaping up to be a pretty good day.

But a final question had lodged in Devon's mind.

"You said this was one of Cromfield's safe houses," he began tentatively, "a place you'd probably come a hundred times before. How could you not remember where it is?"

There was a slight wilting of Gabriel's shoulders, the quietest of sighs.

In hindsight, he'd probably been waiting for the question. The only reason he hadn't gotten it sooner, was because the fox was still fuming at having been *basically abducted in a stolen car*. But there was only so long he could avoid answering. The man had indulged him at every corner of the city, but he'd been trained to seek out the truth of things, just like himself.

They slowed to a stop at a traffic light, idling in the cold.

"Cromfield never trusted us," Gabriel finally answered, surprised by how much it cost him to say the words, "not completely. He didn't trust anyone," he added, as if to defend himself. "He kept most of his research at the lab—buried beneath heaps of stone, kept under lock and key. But there were other things—objects he'd acquired, projects he'd already finished—that he stored in different places. *Things of great value*," he quoted, fingers tightening on the wheel. "Whenever Angel and I would drop something off...he'd erase the location from our memories."

Devon cast a look across the car, staring in utter shock.

Over the years, he'd come to understand the daily atrocities of Jonathon Cromfield a little better. Bits and pieces had slipped out, some things had been told to him directly. But for whatever reason, this struck him as particularly obscene: to forcibly remove a person's memories.

There could be no greater violation. No greater breach of trust.

"I'm sorry," he murmured, not knowing what else to say. He cast another look across the car, but his friend was composed as ever. "How does Mary fit in?"

Something flashed across his face, an emotion gone too quick to identify.

"He didn't know about Mary," he said bluntly, turning towards their street. "One of my few little rebellions." That emotion again, it might have been a smile. "Whenever I knew I'd be dropping something at a safe house, I'd visit Mary on the way over. She'd take the address for safe-keeping."

Take the address?

It took Devon a second to understand.

"She's a nmemokinetic," he murmured in sudden comprehension. "Like Natasha."

Gabriel nodded mutely, rolling to a stop at the curb.

In an uncharacteristic move, he'd parked in front of the fox's house instead of his own. Most days, he delighted in making him walk. Not until much later would Devon remember that he wasn't actually stopping. He needed to deal with the stolen car, before returning home.

"It isn't as bad as you're thinking," he blurted suddenly, flashing a look across the car as if to gauge the fox's expression. "I've had Natasha erase a few."

Normally, Devon took great pride in keeping his emotions in check. But in that moment, there was no disguising his complete and utter shock.

"You have?"

Like what, he wanted to ask. But *that* was a question he'd take to the grave.

Gabriel nodded silently, fingers idling on the wheel.

"You told me...you told me a person should never do that," Devon continued softly. "You said that our memories define us—for better or worse, they make us who we are."

There was a slight pause.

"I never told you that. I said it to Rae."

"I was eavesdropping."

The assassin smiled faintly, but it stilled on his face.

"A few weeks ago, I was training in the Oratory when Krista came with her new baby. She said there were some papers she needed to grab, but I think she just wanted to show the thing off."

Devon nodded silently, he remembered.

"I offered to watch it upstairs so she could talk with Carter, we were playing on the mats. Everything was fine, until someone tossed a fireball. The kid screamed...and I had a panic attack."

The fox raised his eyebrows slowly. "You?"

Gabriel nodded, eyes fixed on a point across the street. "One day, Jason's going to have a baby," he murmured. "One day, I'm going to want to get a full night's sleep. Sometimes I think it's better if...if Natasha erased some of them." There was a lot more he might have said, but he'd reached his limit. Already, he was second-guessing himself, casting another look across the car. "I'm guessing you have some thoughts on the matter."

But Devon merely shook his head. "That's not my place," he said quietly. "I haven't lived through what you've lived through. I haven't seen what you've seen. Chances are, I'd be wanting to erase some memories myself." He opened the car door, but paused in the frame. "I'd only say this: all those memories, all that damage, the darkest things I can imagine...you've managed to turn it into something good."

The assassin let out a breath, fingers drumming on the wheel. "Yeah, I'm a real poster boy for reform—"

"You've saved my life," Devon said bluntly. "You've saved my wife. My children. Those things turned you into the kind of person who could do that. You really asked Natasha?"

Gabriel nodded silently.

"Ok, then I'll ask you one more question and leave it be. If you didn't have those memories...would you have ever met Natasha?"

Chapter 6

Leave it to Devon to ruin a perfectly good day.

Gabriel clenched his teeth as he shot through the city, looking for a place to leave what might have been a perfectly unassuming getaway car. He'd always favored the slow ones if there might be a chase—gave him a chance to test out his skills. But when he considered leaving it at the salvage yard, there was Devon's voice in his head again, telling him to drive the other way.

You're just feeling sentimental because of Mary. Tomorrow, things will be back to normal.

Yes, he hadn't counted on how strongly he'd been affected by seeing the old woman again, embracing in the hallway as if no time had passed. Every time he thought he'd buried those demons, something from his new life pulled them back again, and he found himself thrust more into the fire.

My NEW life, he thought with a spark of frustration. *By now, I've lived it nearly as long as my old one. When am I going to stop calling it that? When am I going to get past this?*

He glanced down in surprise, as there was a buzz in his pocket—removing his leather gloves with his teeth, to answer his phone. A name flashed across the screen, and his face went still.

There were a few people you never wanted calling if you were returning a stolen vehicle.

The London County Correctional Office was one of them.

"Hello?" he said hesitantly, glancing up and down the street.

It was quiet this time of night, even the tourists and the bookies had finally stumbled out of the clubs and tucked themselves into bed. The lights were dark and the city was dreaming.

A robotic voice spoke through the line. "Will you accept a call from the London County Correctional Office?"

Are they taking reservations now?

"Yes," he answered, waiting a bit nervously.

His first thought was Angel, but he knew for a fact that there was a *True Crime* marathon on television that night. His next thought was Jason, but the boy would most likely call his wife.

His last thought was Natasha, but he dismissed that with a smile.

"Mr. Alden?" a familiar voice echoed through the line, one that sounded even more nervous than he was. It paused a second, before stammering a clarification. "It's...it's Alex."

The illegal car rolled to a stop, and Gabriel cut the engine. He sat there a moment, staring at the dark expanse of road in front of him, before answering without inflection.

"Alexander, why are you calling me from jail?"

He could practically see the returning scowl.

"They said you left your wallet," the boy snapped into the phone.

Gabriel waited on the other end, tapping a finger on the receiver.

It was quiet for a few seconds, then the shifter let out a defeated sigh. "Are you going to bail me out, or what?"

Without a second's hesitation, the assassin stepped from the car—leaving the keys with an apologetic note on the dash, as he started walking back up the road.

"I'll bail you out," he answered, "if only for the chance to smack you upside the head." His eyes roved up and down the empty street. "I just need to find myself a cab."

INSTEAD OF GOING DIRECTLY to jail, Gabriel made the shifter wait a little while—taking a taxi back across town and driving there in his own car. By the time he pulled up, the nightshift was already changing, and the guards who'd clocked out were heading to their cars. A few of them waved their hands as the assassin walked past. A few of them teasingly pulled out their handcuffs.

"Don't be ridiculous," he scoffed, breezing past them. "You know those can't hold me."

The gang might have erased all memory of their latest criminal encounter—courtesy of Gabriel's beautiful wife—but they were still frequent visitors. When the chief of police had retired a month before, they'd sent over a dozen bottles of her favorite Spanish wine.

Ten bottles. His sister had refused to participate and kept two for herself.

With a distressing familiarity, he breezed through the double doors and headed towards the front counter—where a man in a navy uniform glanced up in surprise. He needed only a second to recognize the assassin before his face split into a friendly smile.

"You visiting someone? Or checking in?"

I've been spending too much time in this place.

"That's hilarious," Gabriel answered dryly, resting both arms on the counter. "I'm looking for a young man brought in earlier. Dark hair, athletic build. Probably hasn't been making friends."

The man typed a few seconds, then leaned back in his chair. "We got one like that," he answered. "Hastings, Alexander." He flashed a quick look over the screen. "It's not his first offense, and he resisted the arresting officer. Bail's set at five thousand."

Of course it is.

Gabriel rolled his eyes and reached for his wallet, silently cursing whoever had seen fit to give the shifter his phone number. "At this point, we should just start a tab..."

The man chuckled and pushed a button beneath the counter. A harsh bell sounded, and the door swung open to reveal a brightly-lit hall. "You know where it is?"

"I know where it is. Thanks, Jerry."

He strode without hesitation down the corridor, pausing at the end to examine the contents of a vending machine. Finally, when he'd drawn things out long enough, he rounded the corner with a flourish and came to a stop in front of the general holding room. There were thirty or so men lounging behind the bars. Bored out of their minds, most of them repeat offenders. The clock ticked loudly on the wall behind them as they waited for the next steps: a transfer, a phone call, a visit with an overworked and under-paid attorney. Only one of them was sitting at perfect attention, hands curled and feet bouncing, determined to ignore the pointed stares of the rest of the room.

Gabriel kicked the bars with a loud clatter, announcing himself with a smile. "You owe me five thousand pounds, Hastings. We may need to find you a summer job."

Alexander pushed quickly to his feet, hyperaware of the people behind him. The gang might have spent an unhealthy amount of time in lockup, but it was still a novelty to their children. The young man was stressed to the brink—flashing looks at every corner, jumping at every sound.

He stepped swiftly forward so the two might have a private discussion. Then he realized that wouldn't be possible, and hovered uncertainly in front of the bars.

"Sorry, I didn't know who else to call." He made a quick study of Gabriel's face, trying to gauge his mood. "I also figured you'd seen the inside of a jail cell once or twice."

The assassin pursed his lips. "...I'll take that as a compliment."

The truth was, a part of him did. Another part was merely baffled. The shifter had made a minimal effort over the last few years to ingratiate himself into the gang—but there were a few people with whom he'd developed the beginnings of a genuine relationship. Tristan Wardell was near the top of that list, having decided to unofficially mentor the boy. Luke was another. Normally, he would have called one of them. Gabriel wasn't on the list. He would have laughed at the idea.

Why call me—the guy who just beat him senseless at the school gym?

"So, what are we into this time?" he asked, leaning casually against the bars of the cell like they were just another piece of furniture. "Powders? Prostitutes? A general sense of dickery?"

Alexander shifted his weight uncomfortably, feeling the eyes of the people behind him. "I thought you were going to bail me out."

"Already paid up front," the assassin answered lightly, "just figured I'd talk with you first. So are you going to tell me why you're in here? Or will I have to shake it out of you?"

The shifter folded his arms, glaring in silence.

Alright, we can play that game.

Gabriel regarded him a moment, then raised his voice loud enough for the entire precinct to hear. "I don't care how much fun it is, you must *stop* taking your clothes off down by the pier. There are other hobbies, Alexander. You could take up embroidery."

There was a chortle of laughter from the other inmates, and the shifter closed his eyes.

"Are you finished?" he asked through gritted teeth.

No response means yes.

"Alright, I'll take him," Gabriel called over his shoulder. There was a loud *clang*, and the door swung open. "Just so you're aware, this place has a return to sender policy," he added, when the young man slipped through the doors and joined him. "If you're not a bit more forthcoming, I'll drive you straight back here and you can spend the night with all your new friends."

Alexander opened his mouth with a biting response, then flashed an involuntary look over his shoulder. Half a dozen faces loomed back at him, grinning in the fluorescent light.

"...understood."

THE WALKED WITHOUT speaking across the parking lot to the assassin's car—a gleaming new offering straight off a racetrack in Monaco that looked ready to lift into the sky.

Alexander paused by the doors, staring in quiet reverence. "...this is yours?"

The children had been working for the agency several years now, amassing the same kinds of trophies as their parents. But they hadn't been doing it as long, and there were levels of prominence.

Gabriel flashed a look, sliding into the driver's seat. "Touch nothing, change nothing." He flipped on the engine, and the car thrummed to life. "Hastings, I don't even want you to breathe."

The boy grinned in spite of himself, sliding in beside him. "Roger that."

They made a wide turn out of the parking lot and then shot towards downtown, skimming along the roads at such ridiculous speed, every officer who'd waved to the assassin would have been honor-bound to drag him back in chains. There wasn't any talking. There wasn't any lecturing. After a few minutes, the shifter was half-hoping he might simply getting dumped on the curb.

Those hopes were quickly extinguished.

"That's my flat," he called suddenly, pointing to the other side of the road. When the car kept straight ahead, he twisted around in surprise. "That's the exit to my flat—you missed it."

"We're not going to your flat," Gabriel said calmly.

He spun the wheel and cut across two lanes of traffic, flying onto the southern interstate that ran out of the city. There was a cacophony of angry horns from the other drivers, but they'd already passed them. Only a few minutes later, the lights of London were fading in the background, as the shadowy crests and curves of the English countryside loomed up ahead.

Alexander stared in silence out the window, wishing he'd called someone else. "Where are we going?" he finally asked, shooting a look across the car. "Or are you just looking for an easier place to stash my body?"

Gabriel kept his eyes on the road, humming distractedly. "Actually, I prefer to stash my bodies in the city," he replied, drumming his fingers on the wheel. He caught the boy staring, and flashed a smile. "Give those poor coppers something to do."

They pulled onto a private lane about twenty minutes later, rolling to a stop in the faculty parking lot. The gilded towers of Guilder rose up in the distance, painted in moonlight and half-shrouded by mist. It was dark, by then, most everyone on campus was already sleeping.

Gabriel cut the engine, considering his next words. But the shifter beat him to it.

"Why did you bring me here?" he demanded.

I was spoiled with Jason. I would have set this kid on fire.

"I brought you here because we're going to have a little chat," Gabriel answered, forcing an even tone. "I didn't want to do it at your flat, because it might get a little loud. And I don't want to do it in the car, because I might want to rough you up a bit." He waved a hand at the upholstery, opening the door at the same time. "Leather seats."

He got out without another word, leaving the shifter no choice but to follow.

"You might want to rough me up, huh?" Alexander asked, eyeing him carefully. After their confrontation in the school gym, he'd hesitated a great deal before dialing the assassin's number. But in a strange way, it was what had prompted him to call. "Why didn't we just go to your house?"

"You're not welcome at my house."

At that point, Gabriel started pacing across the moonlit lawns, glancing occasionally around the campus as he went. Truth be told, he didn't have much of a plan. He'd been feeling unsettled already when he'd received the shifter's call, and hadn't yet been able to gather his thoughts. He paused beneath a grove of trees, restless and searching, then turned abruptly to the nearest cottage.

"In here," he said quietly, picking the lock. "Wipe your shoes."

Alexander froze incredulously behind him, watching as the door sprang free. "Whose cottage is this?"

"Don't worry about it," Gabriel answered, pushing the door open wider. "Just get inside."

The shifter planted on the doormat, gesturing to the Oratory. "Why don't we just go to your office—"

"*Shut your bloody mouth*," Gabriel commanded in exasperation, grabbing his wrist and yanking him through the door. He locked it behind them, then led the shifter into the kitchen—pulling a towel from a drawer and gesturing to the sink. "For your hands."

Alexander looked down in surprise at the ink smeared over his fingers, as Gabriel swept into the sparsely-decorated living room—pacing from one side to another. He hadn't counted on adding another item to the day's agenda. If he was being honest, he might not have trusted himself to see it through. No matter how much time elapsed, his head was still spinning with the din of the gambling hall, his neck was still tingling where Mary's frail arms had circled around the back.

And always, Devon's infernal question whispered in his ears.

'If you didn't have those memories...would you have ever met Natasha?'

"I can't believe you just broke in here," Alexander muttered, joining him in the living room and examining the haphazard clatter on the shelves. He came to a pause beside a wooden crate filled with straw packaging. "Are those hand grenades?! Seriously, man, who's staying here—"

"Don't worry about it," Gabriel snapped, pointing to the sofa. "Just sit down and shut up. I don't know what moment of insanity led to your arrest, but before we get started—"

"*Gabriel?*"

The pair turned around to see a sleepy-looking man standing in the hallway. Workout shorts, mismatched socks, and bed-tousled hair. He blinked slowly, like he might still be dreaming.

"This isn't a good time, Jack. I'm having a teachable moment."

There was a confounded pause.

"...in my living room?"

"The school owns the cottage," Gabriel snapped. "Go back to bed."

The man rolled his eyes and shuffled back down the hall, muttering under his breath. *"Prick."*

Alexander lifted his eyebrows, trying to hold back a smile. "We're having a teachable moment?"

"We're about to," Gabriel answered, perching on the coffee table in front of him. His arms draped over his knees as he leaned closer, staring the shifter in the eyes. "Why were you in jail?"

He was prepared to go nine rounds. He was prepared to make a thorough mess of Jack's living room, and use whatever threats he needed to. But the young man gave him a simple reply.

"Shoplifting."

Gabriel leaned back with a touch of surprise. "Shoplifting," he repeated slowly. "Okay."

Not what I was expecting.

A sudden quiet fell over the room as each of them considered the next steps. What had been meant to be a stern confrontation, now felt distressingly close to a conversation that might happen between father and son. After a few moments, Gabriel abandoned the coffee table and sat beside him on the sofa. A few moments after that, Alexander flashed him a sideways glance.

"Are you going to start yelling at me?" he asked quietly.

The assassin shook his head, staring at a fixed point on the floor. "No yelling. I've shoplifted plenty of times myself." He considered another moment, then returned the boy's look. "Never been caught, though."

Alexander warmed with the barest of smiles. "Guess my heart wasn't in it."

Guess not.

They sat there a while longer as the moon passed silently above them, mulling over the day's events, wondering how the day might finally end. Then Gabriel pushed abruptly to his feet.

"You're going to tell me a story," he said. "Those six transfers we got from the Abbey—the ones you nearly beat to death on the front lawn—you're going to tell me what happened to them."

If you'd asked that morning, he would have sworn the boy would refuse. He might have refused that very evening—making some sarcastic comment and jutting up his chin. But a single truth had passed between them, and that was never enough. A single truth invited more.

No matter how difficult it might be.

Gabriel watched that difficulty pass across the boy's face, like watching the ripples from a stone tossed in a well. He could do nothing to control it. Each rising crest of emotion flared over him like a fever, leaving behind its particular mark. He took a deep breath, but found no solace.

Instead of taking another, he dove in—stringing out the tale one painful word at a time.

"The same thing that always happens," he answered in a strange, quiet voice. "They got swept into a system that should have helped them, they got forgotten by everyone who was supposed to remember. They just...ceased to exist." He went quiet for a moment, staring at his hands. "You ever spent time in a foster home?"

Gabriel shook his head in silence.

"Of course you haven't," the shifter corrected himself, "what am I saying? Well, yours might have been worse, but I'm guessing a few of the general principles are the same. Time passes differently in those places. It...creeps. Sometimes it's barely moving, other times you can't believe how much has passed. The worst part is, it doesn't matter. Because nothing ever changes. The scenery changes. The people are shuffled in and out. But you...? You're just standing still."

His eyes drifted out the window, like he could see the cottages on the other side. They were veiled by trees, but shifters had sharp eyes. He found the one he was looking for, staring in the dark.

"A bunch of us snuck up to the roof one night," he continued softly, "we made ourselves this promise. We said that if any of us ever made it out of the system, we'd come back for the others. We wouldn't just leave them there, to *rot*." A look of true pain swept over him, burning like a dying fire. "I got out of that place almost ten years ago...I never went back."

Gabriel bowed his head, giving the words a chance to settle.

How many times had he and Angel had similar conversations? How many whispered promises had they made? They seemed almost holy in the dark, sacred and binding.

Then the sun rose the next morning, and nothing was the same.

"You couldn't have gone back," he said softly. "You were a recruit with zero clearance. By the time the dust settled with Dorian, most of those kids would have already aged out—"

"I know all that," Alexander interrupted, eyes on his knees. He stayed like that a moment before shaking his head. "But let me tell you...I didn't try very hard to get back."

Another silence fell between them. The story had reached its end.

Gabriel stared at the boy without speaking, taking in all those details he'd missed before, the details so many had missed. It was suddenly easy to see the pain behind his scowls, the cold truth that cut short every laugh and twisted his smiles with guilt. It was suddenly easy to understand why ever since the transfers had arrived, he'd been systematically imploding his new life. Quitting his job, pushing away his friends, landing himself in jail for something as silly as a stolen piece of gum.

If that hadn't worked, Gabriel was willing to bet he'd have set the entire city on fire—just to feel the burn of it, just to bring the wreckage down upon his own head.

He opened his mouth, but words failed him. Then a voice drifted out of the bedroom.

"*You guys want me to put on some coffee...?*"

"Not now, Jack!" he shouted angrily.

Alexander hurled a pillow down the hall.

When it landed, the spell was broken. They were both smiling. Subdued, but smiling. And for the first time since they'd rolled into the parking lot, Gabriel had a plan.

"Listen, you weren't there for them then? You be there for them now." He pushed to his feet. "I'm putting you in charge of their transition. You're going to act as their handler."

Alexander's smile vanished into a look of pure horror. "What?" he cried, rising as well. "I can't do that! Weren't you listening—"

"I *was* listening," Gabriel interrupted. "And I am telling you as someone who knows...there is no running from something like this. There is no amount of damage you can do to yourself that's going to take it away. You face it on both feet, or it crushes you. There isn't a third option."

The shifter looked at him for a split second, then started shaking his head. "No, absolutely not. You can't make me do that, Gabriel. It's bad enough you won't let me quit—"

"Do you know how many of those stories I have?" the assassin countered. "Do you know how many years it took for me to go back? Maybe if I'd tried a little harder, that bus full of kids wouldn't have slipped off a bridge in Jakarta. Maybe if I'd caught on a little faster, that apartment complex wouldn't have blown up in Guam. Maybe, maybe..." He trailed into silence, shaking his head. "Maybe if I'd driven across town a little faster...Jason's father might still be alive."

They stared at each other, holding in the same breath.

"You can't live your life on a maybe," Gabriel finished quietly. "And you can't outrun your guilt by writing it off as regret. You want redemption, Hastings? You have to earn it." He pointed blindly out the window. "And you can start by helping those people right over there."

The words hung in the air between them, waiting for resolution.

"I'm appointing you as their handler. Do you accept?"

Alexander lifted his eyes, drew in a breath. "Yes, I accept."

Gabriel nodded slowly, brimming with pride. "Good." It was quiet a few seconds, then he cocked his head to the door. "Now get out of here, Hastings. You're trespassing."

Alexander bit his lip, fighting back a true smile. "I learned from the best."

THEY HEADED OUTSIDE together, tightening their coats with a shiver as they stepped onto the frosted grass. It crunched beneath their boots, patches of silver and shadow in the moonlight. It would be snowing before long. Already, the first tiny flakes were starting to fall.

"You need a ride home?" Gabriel asked, lifting his head to the sky. "I was going to train for a while, but if you wanted to head back—"

"Mr. Alden?"

He glanced over his shoulder to see a slim figure heading towards them—the silhouette of a young woman, materializing from the shadows. She'd been wandering around the campus, hoping to see a few of those snowflakes herself. But she'd paused when the door to one of the cottages swung open, piercing the darkness with a splinter of light. She'd been surprised to recognize one of the men who'd stepped outside. She was too far away still, to see the other.

"I thought it was you," she said with a rare smile, moving closer. Her long hair spilled loose around her shoulders, catching the silver light. "I just drank the last of that tea—"

She stopped abruptly upon seeing Alexander, the smile freezing on her face.

"—what's he doing here?"

The shifter froze where he was standing, looking like he'd give anything in the world to be sitting back in jail. He was about to say as much—that bristling defensiveness rising to the tip of his tongue—but he caught himself, forcing a cordial smile instead.

"Hello, Elise."

Gabriel stepped between them with a quick smile. "He actually works here," he teased, trying to keep things light. "Something you repeatedly refuse, in spite of our sparkling hospitality." He paused a moment before continuing. "If you ever do decide to head into the Oratory—Alex will help you. I've asked him to be your mentor."

She turned from one to the other, looking like the devil herself. "And why would you do a thing like that?" she asked in a whisper. Before the assassin could answer, she pointed a finger at Alexander's chest. "He offered you a promotion, because he doesn't know any better. But we both know the truth about you. Don't we, *Alex*?"

Beneath the gathering clouds, the shifter went very pale.

"I've said I was sorry, *so many times*." His eyes found hers, shining and raw. "I've sent you letters. I've come by the house. If you would just let me explain—"

"There is *nothing* to explain!" she hissed, jabbing that finger into his chest. "Do you hear me?! There is *nothing* you can say that can make it any better! You want to spin me some story, Hastings? How about I just do it for you. You got your chance to leave—and you left. That's it."

Gabriel stood between them, feeling like there was a chapter he'd missed.

Yes, the shifter had been transferred to Guilder. And yes, he'd hopped on the bus. But he hadn't been alone. His twin sister had gone with him. Another shifter had gone as well. This girl wasn't railing against either of them. It was Alexander—*specifically*. His eyes strayed to the mark she'd left on his chest, wondering what they'd been to each other before he had gone.

"It wasn't that simple," Alexander breathed, his voice whispering over the grass. "No part of this has been simple. And if you think there's been a single day that I haven't..." His arm reached towards her before lowering back to his side. "El, please can we just—"

But the girl wasn't in the mood for favors. She wasn't in the mood to talk at all.

Without stopping to consider the ramifications of what she was doing, she squared her shoulders and levelled another finger at his chest. There was something different about this one, a kind of tingling in the air around it. One that was only too obvious to those who knew the signs.

Gabriel knew the signs. He didn't know the girl's ink, but he knew the signs.

Without stopping to consider the ramifications of what *he* was doing, he stepped right in front of Alexander—absorbing whatever she'd been aiming into his own chest.

For a solitary moment, the world hung in suspension. Then it vanished with a great rushing sound as the image before him changed. He remembered throwing out a hand for balance. He remembered being struck with a final thought: This is why she doesn't tell people about her tatù.

Then he was standing in a memory. His own memory, narrated by his own voice.

I was sixteen, maybe seventeen. Couldn't have been any older than that, because I didn't have a scar below my collarbone. I'd get it that Christmas. For now, the skin was smooth and unmarked.

There was a sound of voices further in the cave, but nothing closer. The other people who'd found themselves in the grip of my employer, the ones who occasionally shared our tunnels, had learned to keep their distance. They didn't often speak to Angel or me, but that might have been Cromfield's doing. He liked to make lines between us. He liked those lines to run straight to him. But years of toiling away in the shadows had bred a certain familiarity. I remember when those barriers started to shrink. It was a shortly after I'd saved a group of them from a South American firing squad—they'd warmed to me in a hurry after that. Of course, I was unable to warm to them in return. It had been too many years seeing their faces, hearing their voices. They'd witnessed too many atrocities, spent too many hours at his right hand. I kept them at arm's length—I didn't know how to do any different. He wouldn't have let me if I did.

A few of them kept trying, though. They used to tease me about my hair. Goldilocks, they would call me.

I'd completely forgotten about that until now...

Gabriel staggered backwards, raising a trembling hand like a shield. The image was flickering, but a part of him had broken free. Already, it was gripping him. Trying to drag him back.

"What are you going?" he gasped, trying to keep the girl in focus. "Make it stop."

Alexander was shouting behind him. "Turn it off, Elise!"

She stared without expression. The world went dark once again.

I finished the last of my cereal and headed into the hall, ready for whatever the day had in store. I was meant to be processing a new prisoner, but Cromfield led me the opposite direction—to a small alcove that had been left empty after the hydrokinetic who'd been imprisoned there died. I could still see the marks of his fingernails on the wall.

"Shut the door."

I'd learned to fear such requests; nothing good ever came from them. Nevertheless, I moved quickly to do as he asked, waiting with perfect obedience as he rummaged in the corner and returned with a strange-look-

ing metal. It had changed a great deal since being delivered a few days before—flattening and widening into a gleaming slab.

"Do you remember what this is?" he asked, never looking away.

I nodded faintly, my eyes travelling over it.

There was a story some merchant had sold him. A story about a metal discovered in some rare mines that could sink through a person's bones. They were calling it something stupid. Tambor, I think. Angel had made a joke about a tambourine. We'd laughed and forgotten it. That had been much of our relationship then. Anyway, this metal was special, the man who'd sold it claimed. Prophesied by some ancient civilization.

Of course, this caught my employer's ear.

He was quite taken with prophecies at the moment. If someone had asked me then to describe him—that was the phrase my teenage brain might have come up with: *He was quite taken with prophecies at the moment.*

You see, a certain person had recently come back into his life. A girl whose name we'd grown up hearing. Rae Kerrigan. She had just moved to England. They had been fated, he'd said proudly. It was their destiny to meet.

All this to say, he was in just the mood for some prophesied stone.

"It's called tambor, isn't it?" I said quietly.

I always spoke quietly around him, taking up as little space as possible. Like he might someday notice. Like he might someday realize how convenient and useful I was, and things might start to change.

It's funny now, how I used to think those kinds of things.

He nodded to himself, turning it over speculatively. "There's nothing heavier on the planet. I must use my greatest strength tatù just to wield this small amount." His eyes glowed in the gleam of it.

A metal strong enough to sink through a person's bones.

He was a practical man, but he liked to believe himself to be fantastical. He believed a great many things about himself. He certainly believed a great many things about me.

"Lie down," he said.

I stared at him. We were standing in the middle of the floor.

It wasn't that I refused—I'd been leaping at the man's commands since I was old enough to walk. My body simply wasn't obeying, the muscles had locked up the second I'd seen that dangerous curiosity stirring in his eyes.

"Lie down, Gabriel."

I remembered the surprise on his face when he had to say it twice.

It felt like someone had placed a bag over my head. I could scarcely hear the sound of my own breaths, my ears were raw and ringing. My mouth went dry, but before I could try to speak, he was moving towards me across the room. His hands lifted and I braced for a strike, but he put them on my shoulders—staring intently into my eyes.

"Nothing bad is going to happen. Trust me."

Like an obedient dog, I lay on the ground at his feet. He brought over the stone and knelt beside me, his face rigid with concentration at having carried it thus far. It had been thinned and hammered, curving into a broader shape.

He'd done this himself, he said. To distribute the weight, so it would be safe.

I nodded faintly.

Nothing about this felt safe.

The cold floor pressed into my shoulders as he lowered it towards me. It looked like a piece of old-fashioned armor—something a knight would have worn. I used to be obsessed with those stories. I didn't recognize that boy anymore. When it touched my skin, some part of me bolted. I couldn't explain it. My body had stamped out those impulses years ago. But this was something more urgent, more primal. Something I wasn't yet willing to understand.

He looked into my eyes. "Trust me."

He wasn't using persuasion. That was a story I'd tell myself later on.

I closed my eyes and he lay the plate across my chest, watching closely all the while. A fractured gasp burst from my lips and my eyes flew open *again—stunned by the sheer weight of it. It felt absurd that the only thing stopping it from reaching the floor was my trembling ego and the strength of my ribs. Neither was up to the task.*

My eyes drifted up, he was waiting for an assessment.

"It's—" Another breath tore from me, like an invisible hand had ripped it from my chest. Beads of sweat trickled through my hair, and my legs thrashed in spite of themselves. "It's—"

"Don't move," he commanded.

My body went instantly still, like I'd been given a drug.

The tambor punished me for it, pressing itself into the very limits of my skin. There would be blood soon, lots of it. Then would come the muffled crack of bones.

He knelt above me, scribbling down notes.

"Can you sense the metal?" he asked.

It was madness that he would ask something further. The pressure was great enough that I could not have remembered my own name. Nevertheless, I tried to do as he asked—reaching out with my tatù.

"It's strange—"

"But you can sense it?" he prompted.

I nodded miserably, understanding the nature of my hopeless task.

"You must find a grip on it," he instructed, peering down like a professor in front of the class. "The man was right—this much weight will sink right through your chest if you don't stop it. You'll die," he added unnecessarily.

My eyes watered and I nodded quickly, trying to pull in a breath. His hand was still gripping it, I hadn't realized that before—wedged between my skin and the plate. He slid away his fingers, and bones start to crack.

Damn, that hurts!

I let out a broken grasp, pushing wildly against it with both hands. All my desperation and strength, but it didn't move a single inch. It pinned me like a butterfly, legs thrashing against the floor.

"I can't—"

It sank a hair deeper, and I let out an involuntary cry.

"It takes air to scream," he said calmly, "and you can't have much left. Use what's left and summon your ink. It's the reason I chose you for this. Because you're special—the only one who might rise to the challenge."

The words were like a drug to me. I rallied my strength and tried again. But it was like trying to hold back the tides. No matter what I did, how much I leveled against it, the thing was breaking through me, one bone at a time.

"Bear it, Gabriel. Do not disappointment me."

Tears were trickling down my face. My shirt was damp with blood. A rib cracked, then another. Two neat fractures, buckling them towards my lungs. I gasped again, fingers scrabbling against the edge.

"I can't—"

Another rib. Another scream.

He leaned over me curiously, like he was wondering if there was someone who could.

"Bear it, Gabriel. Lesser men than you have borne it."

But I couldn't do it. No one could.

My eyes blurred over as I lifted them to his face. But I'll never quite forget what I saw. For better or worse, the man had raised me. He'd bought me clothes when I stretched through the ones I was wearing. I'd learned to toddle around those shadowy halls. For years, I had served him faithfully. My entire life had been dedicated to the cause.

And now, he was going to watch me die.

Because he was curious about a merchant's story. Because I wasn't worth enough to save.

But in that moment, I realized something about myself as well.

I realized I wanted to live.

Even now, I can scarcely describe what happened to me in that moment. It was a welling of energy unlike anything I'd felt before—a preternatural focus that comes in the moment between life and death. Instead of balking at the strangeness or gasping again for air, I leaned into it—letting the feeling consume me completely. It was like finding a friend in the stillness, a light in the dark. It could move, when I could not. It could reach past those dim walls, past that unholy plate, and grab it in a way my trembling fingers could never manage. It found easy purchase and swelled like an extension of my own consciousness. I could almost see the color of it, the pulsing waves of strength.

With a mighty cry, I heaved a corner of it away from my body—panting for air like a man surfacing from the depths of the sea. It lasted only a moment and no longer, but a moment was all I needed. The second it was in the air, Cromfield reached for it himself—grabbing on with both hands and tossing it into the corner of the room.

It clattered into a deafening silence. My breaths came in shattered gasps.

"You did it."

My eyes ventured upwards again, resting on Cromfield's face. It was worse than I could have imagined. He wasn't impressed, or relieved, or even particularly pleased by the outcome. He was surprised. He didn't think I would.

And he made me do it anyway.

A quiet whimper stole past my lips, as I curled onto my side—clutching weakly at my crushed ribs. I was still crying, but I didn't notice that at the time. I was still bleeding, but I didn't notice that either. In a rare moment of...what? Absentmindedness? Compassion? He reached down and stroked a hand through my hair.

"That was very good," he said quietly.

My breathing slowed and my heartbeat quickened.

I leaned without thinking into his hand.

"We'll try again tomorrow."

By the time my eyes opened, he was already gone. There was nothing but my broken ribs, that cursed plate, and the promise of tomorrow. My cheek burned where his hand had touched it. I buried my face in my arm.

And cried, and cried, and cried.

Gabriel's eyes opened for a single moment, then he dropped to his knees.

"Mr. Alden," Alexander gasped, dropping with him. For a full minute, he'd been clutching the assassin's hand—keeping him steady. "Are you all right?"

It was a ridiculous question. The man could barely speak.

"What did you do to him?" the shifter demanded instead, shooting a vicious glare at the girl standing before them. "Elise, what did you do?!"

She crouched hesitantly on the other side, pale as a sheet. "I'm sorry," she mumbled. "It just got away from—"

He shoved her away, out of reach. "Get back to your cottage," he commanded. "*Now*, Callaway. I'll speak with you later."

She staggered to her feet and scrambled backwards—pausing at the edge of the waning light to cast a tearful look over her shoulder. By the time he turned back to the assassin, she was gone.

"...Mr. Alden?"

Gabriel opened his eyes slowly, still feeling like he couldn't pull in a full breath. The cave was gone, and the ceiling had opened to a sky full of stars. He stared at them in a daze.

A hand lifted to his ribs. "What the hell just happened?" he breathed.

Alexander knelt beside him, a hand placed awkwardly on his back. "It's her ink," he said with an apologetic grimace. "There's a reason she doesn't ..." He trailed off, shaking his head. "We should get you to the infirmary. I'll take your—"

But Gabriel was already pushing to his feet, ignoring the shifter's attempts to help him. The ground swayed beneath him, but his balance was returning by the second. When he heard Alexander shouting behind him, he waved him off—staggering towards the parking lot.

"It's all right," he called back, still bracing a hand against his ribs. They didn't hurt, nothing hurt. But he couldn't lower his hand. "Everything's fine, I just..." He quickened his pace, throwing a look over his shoulder. Alexander was frozen a few steps behind. "You can get back to the city?"

The boy nodded, looking like he was being torn in half.

"Yeah, I'll...I'll be fine. Don't worry about that." He hesitated a moment, forcing himself to continue. "Mr. Alden, you really shouldn't drive. Can I take you home? Or call someone, at least?"

Gabriel shook his head quickly, already nearing the lot. "I'm fine. I'll see you later, Alex."

The shifter called something in return, but he never heard it. The second he reached his car, he used his ink to open the door and threw himself inside. It locked behind him. There was no one else in sight. With a trembling hand, he cupped his mouth—trying to stop himself from screaming.

The worst part wasn't the memory, he'd lived that moment before. It wasn't the pain, or the fear, or that academic curiosity that haunted his every breath. The worst part of the story, was how he would tell it—if someone had asked him. How he would frame each moment differently, painting them in a slightly better light. He hadn't lay down of his own free will—who would do such a thing?

The man had persuaded him. He'd also caught the plate, promised Gabriel he would be safe.

But he couldn't think about that now. He couldn't think about anything except his own shattering breaths. Those calculating, curious eyes sweeping over him.

The way he'd leaned into Cromfield's hand.

Chapter 7

It's beginning to look a lot like Christmas...

Devon hummed under his breath, as he jogged across the street—pleased as punch by the thick layer of ice that cracked beneath his shoes. The weather had been playing with them before, sometimes a little rain, sometimes a little sun, but *this* was an English winter. It had snowed in the night, and everywhere he looked, the world had been covered in a heavy blanket of white. The trees were drooping with the weight on their branches, the roads that ribboned his fair city were an ivory seam. The houses looked like something from a postcard, tucked amidst their frosted gardens, smeared with the same thick frosting as everything else. *Gingerbread houses*, that was what James used to call them when he was little. He didn't understand they were something you made, he thought they were something that happened. After so many years, Devon was starting to think it himself.

He picked up the pace with a little smile, crossing the strip of grass that ran along the center of the road before coming to a sudden stop on the sidewalk.

He took one step, then another—staring with a frown.

There were precious few things that he and Gabriel could agree upon, but cars was one of them. No matter what other quarrels shook them, the assassin's collection was nearly as impressive as his own. They were reverent in their ministrations, careful in their treatment. But the crowning jewel of his congregation was parked haphazardly—two wheels on the road, two wheels on the curb.

Devon cast a quick glance over his shoulder, making sure his neighbors still slept, then he lifted it carefully back to the street. The snow creased with a heavy groove, lingering as evidence, and he smeared it even with his boot—lifting his eyes curiously to the little cottage.

What are you up to...?

It was scarcely after dawn, but the fox had no illusion that his friend was awake. Nor did he have the slightest hesitation as he pulled a key from his pocket and slipped it into the lock. He'd made one specially, after the incident at his own house with the nettles. If the assassin had given himself permission to come and go freely, then Devon would do the same.

"Gabriel?" he called, when he stepped inside.

Natasha was away on assignment, he'd signed the order himself. The house was dark and cold without her. The assassin hadn't turned on any lights, not even a heater.

Devon flipped it on as he walked past, stepping carefully into the hall.

He found him almost immediately, sitting on the ground outside Jason's old room. His legs were splayed in front of him, as though he'd sank down without warning, and his eyes were wide and vacant—staring blankly at the opposing wall. A spark of involuntary panic quickened the fox's blood, but he heard a heartbeat. Slow, and constant. He paused at the entry, wishing he'd knocked.

"Gabriel?" he tried again, even softer this time.

He had learned it was better to speak softly and announce himself, rather than take this particular friend by surprise. Bad things happened when Gabriel was surprised.

And he was usually armed.

But there was no surprising him that morning, there didn't seem to be any reaching him. He hadn't moved in the slightest, at the fox's voice. He'd yet to blink his eyes.

Devon moved slowly towards him, crouching to the ground by his feet. With a look of extreme caution, he reached a gentle hand to his friend's ankle, giving him a delicate shake. "Gabriel?"

The assassin drew in a deep breath and roused himself, blinking quickly, as though some part of him had been asleep. He stared around for a moment, then lifted his eyes to Devon. "What time is it?" he asked in confusion.

The fox regarded him intently, trying to keep his own face clear of concern. There was a rising welt upon his cheek, and he was wearing yesterday's clothing. A puddle of melted ice had formed beneath his shoes, staining the wood below them. A bracing hand was lifted to his ribs.

"It's, uh...it's almost seven." He paused a moment before that concern leaked through and he pressed a little farther. "Have you been sitting here all night?"

Gabriel pushed to his feet in a lithe motion, taking a second to orient himself, before noticing the puddle on the floor. He blinked in a kind of mindless surprise, then took off his jacket and dropped it on top—turning around and limping stiffly towards the kitchen.

Devon sopped up the water before heading after him.

"Are you okay?" he asked in spite of himself, watching every step.

The assassin nodded wordlessly, turning on a light. He winced against the sudden shine and flipped it off again—turning instead to the refrigerator. "What are you doing here?"

The fox hesitated, feeling the papers stuffed in his coat. "We have our debrief today, remember? For getting that address?" His cheeks colored with a flush. "I know it's a little stupid, since it was just two of us. But the protocol says—"

"I'm sorry, what?"

He glanced up to see Gabriel staring at him by the open refrigerator, looking like a part of him was still asleep. Devon reached for the papers, then stopped himself halfway there.

"The debrief, for yesterday. Did you forget?"

The assassin stared another moment before nodding quickly. "Right, sorry." He combed back his hair with a tired sigh, glancing helplessly towards the chilled shelves, but seemed unable to form a coherent thought. "Do you want to eat something?"

The fox shook his head, studying him curiously. "I'm fine. Shall we get started?"

Gabriel waved blindly for him to continue, abandoning the idea of breakfast and heading towards the coffeemaker instead. Instead of pouring himself a cup of whatever he'd brewed the night before, he simply took the pot, cradling it delicately as he came to stand beside a window.

"We got to the docks around zero six hundred," Devon began routinely. "Approximately twenty to twenty-five people already present. Fishermen, mostly, but there were a few—"

"It snowed, huh?" Gabriel interrupted softly, staring into the street. "It's pretty." He stared another moment, then glanced over his shoulder. "Want to do this outside?"

Devon paused uncertainly, glancing down at his notes. "Uh...yeah, we could do that. It's a little cold," he added.

Gabriel nodded absentmindedly, missing the obvious cues. "You want a jacket?"

The fox stared a second longer, then his eyes warmed with a little smile. "Sure, thanks."

Without another word, he followed the assassin to the back door—smiling again when the coffee pot was left distractedly on a bookshelf. Gabriel handed him one of the jackets hanging on the rack, glancing back in surprise when the fox looked it over, then traded it for another.

"You don't like that one?" he asked.

Devon shook his head. "I've never liked that one."

"Really. Huh." Gabriel slipped it over his own shoulders, and they stepped outside—settling on the patio furniture and running their eyes along the smooth snowbanks that had encased the yard.

After a few seconds, the assassin shivered. "It's cold," he murmured.

Devon bit his lip. "Yeah."

They exchanged a quick look.

"Well...we're outside already," Gabriel declared.

The fox snorted with laughter, reaching again for his notes. "Let's just get through this, yeah?"

He started reading through what he had so far, making little annotations in the margins and pretending things were normal, as Gabriel sat in silence beside him—trailing a finger in the snow. A minute went past, then another. A bird landed on a fencepost, puffing out its icy wings.

Devon flipped the page, scanning down through a list.

"So I'm guessing you don't want me to include the name Coventry Hall. I'm also guessing you'd rather we skip over the bit about Mary, or at least give her an alias. Is there a different name you'd like written? Or are you fixed on the idea of a geriatric chemist?"

Silence.

"Gabriel?"

The assassin lifted his head, utterly lost. "Hmm?"

Devon lowered the pen, staring across the table.

The two hadn't had the easiest time acclimating to one another. Of all the friends, theirs was undoubtedly the most difficult road. And while they'd made great strides in crossing those bridges, at times like this, there remained a distance between them. One Devon had never learned to cross.

Give him a beat. He clearly needs one.

"Do you want a different name in the official report?" he prompted. "Other than Mary?"

Gabriel's lips parted uncertainly, then closed again. "Dev, I'm sorry, can we do this a different time?"

The fox stared back in surprise, then slipped the papers into his pocket. "Yeah, sure."

They sat there for a while, watching the bird hop from fencepost to fencepost, shivering occasionally in the icy chill.

After a few minutes, Devon glanced across the table. "Are you ready for tomorrow?"

They had decided to take a day before going to the safe house. Given the change that had come over his friend, he was deeply grateful to have suggested it. Perhaps they should take two?

But Gabriel merely nodded, staring into the cloudy sky. "Always," he answered quietly.

The wind picked up again, and snow started to fall.

WHAT THE HECK WAS THAT about?

Devon flew down the frosted roads to Guilder, cursing every time the wheels of his car slipped on the ice. The snow had lost all its charm for him—around the same time he'd been forced to immerse himself in suffocating silence, wondering what on earth was the matter with his friend.

Most days, he would ask his wife.

Much as he hated to admit it, the two shared a special connection, and she could save the assassin from the shadows that plagued him better than most. But Rae had been either working or sleeping the last few days she'd spent in London, and wouldn't have the faintest idea. Odds were, she'd say it was an eating disorder, chide him for trespassing, and force-feed the man some lunch.

Not a bad idea, given the general state of things.

He took a hairpin turn down the narrow lane that led to the school, sliding a few meters into the surrounding field, before speeding off again into the trees.

It wasn't the last mission that bothered him. It was the one that was coming next.

He should have known better than to send the assassin back to his old haunts. He should have sent someone undercover, or just gone by himself. Of course, Gabriel would never have gone along with the idea—and he didn't much fancy having to explain the need for raspberry strudel on an official case report. But the man had been spinning off the rails ever since they'd discovered that strange metal at the museum. Devon kept waiting for things to get better.

They were getting decidedly worse.

And now we're going to an old safe house of Cromfield's. His eyes clouded with worry as he rolled into the parking lot. *A place that's been repeatedly deleted from his memory.*

He cut the engine, sitting in silence.

A fact that he's neglected to tell us until now.

His pulse quickened and his mouth soured with the taste of adrenaline. He leaned back against the headrest, staring blankly through the windshield, trying to slow his breaths. It wasn't the first time he'd been caught off guard by some horror in his friend's past—something that Gabriel had written off as normal, but kept the others awake at night. The first time Rae had tearfully shared the story of how he'd been dragged to the cave in the first place, the fox's vision had clouded with such belated rage, he'd been half-inclined to resurrect Cromfield and strangle him all over again.

But the man was dead and buried, the past was buried with him. It was only the shadows that remained. Whispering and creeping, making tiny cracks in things he'd thought were steady.

In *people* he'd thought were steady.

I guess we can never know for sure.

He got out of the car in a streak of movement, flying across the snowy lawns at supernatural speed. Most days, he made himself walk at a regular pace. It was less unsettling to the people around him. But his nerves were jumping and his pulse was racing. He wanted to get out of the cold.

He appeared as if by magic at the Oratory doors, startling a group of shifters who had just emerged from the other side. He flashed an apologetic grimace, waving in greeting, then reached for the handle himself—before stopping just as fast.

Do I want to go in there? Really?

Instead of answering the question, he reached instinctively into his pocket—pulling out his phone. His finger pressed a button and he raised it to his ear.

A voice answered a second later. "Hey, you're up early!"

He let out a slow breath, staring at the doors. "I have a psychic question for you: if I walk into the Oratory right now, are a dozen people going to mob me the second I step inside? With questions and requests? A problematic swarm?"

The door opened a second later and Julian appeared in the frame. "It's a distinct possibility," he replied, phone still pressed against his ear.

Devon hung up with a grin. "What are you doing here? I thought you were heading back to Brussels."

"Change of plans," the psychic answered easily, beckoning him inside. If there had been a crowd of people preparing to mob him, they scattered at the sight. "Figured I'd spend the morning in here, get in some practice with an inhibitor."

The fox perked up immediately, desperate for anything that wasn't below ground. "Want some help?"

Julian's eyebrows lifted in surprise. "You have the time?"

"Jules, we're *partners*," Devon replied seriously, clasping both his shoulders. "Now and always. There will never come a day that I won't make the time."

There was a speculative pause.

"You're avoiding the office, aren't you?"

"I'd *really* love to stay up here."

The psychic laughed and led the way into the Oratory, waving to a couple of people who called out to him from the mats. Devon trailed in his shadow, immensely relieved not to be making any impromptu speeches, or heading off any impromptu rebellions. If he could make it through an entire session without being asked for his signature, he'd lay down and kiss the floor.

"Since I have you here, I feel like I should take advantage—spar for a while," Julian said lightly, though he reached for a bucket of inhibitors. "Who knows when I might lose you to another elusive shadow organization? It's bad enough I had to sit by myself while Miranda cut my hair."

Devon's head snapped up in alarm. "Did you get a haircut without me?"

Julian shot a sarcastic look over his shoulder. "What do you think?"

No, you'd never do that alone.

The fox nodded swiftly, feeling his pulse settle back into a normal rhythm. A chorus of happy voices echoed beneath the domed ceiling, as his eyes swept slowly over the room.

"This might be a dumb question," he began quietly, "but you can't see anything they're doing, can you? This shadow organization?"

The psychic flashed a wry grin. "Why would you think that's a dumb question?"

Devon chuckled under his breath, following him around the mats.

Despite his attempts to fly below the radar, those clairvoyant eyes had made Julian Decker rather famous. At this point, he was probably the greatest natural deterrent the supernatural world had ever seen. Not since the PC's old president, Royce Masters, had the criminal underworld had such a perfect reason to give the Privy Council and all its agents the widest possible berth.

That, and my wife.

Instead of dominating the practice mats, as was their custom, the two made their way over to a long bench that ran along the side of the room. They swung over a leg and placed the bucket of inhibitors between them. Devon reached into his pocket as Julian slipped one around his neck.

"Alright, smarty." The fox held up a coin, making sure the psychic could see it clearly, before hiding it behind his back. There was a theatric shuffling, then his face went still. "Which hand?"

Julian stared back without expression. "Not sure. Can I see it again?"

Devon laughed, but kept his position—trying to control his face. "Could be the right, could be the left. You'll never know...*unless you open your mind.*"

The psychic snorted with laughter, fiddling with the inhibitor. "I should never have let you help."

"Nonsense," Devon said briskly, straightening to attention. "This is a good idea. We should have started trying to crack these things years ago."

Since the psychic had mastered the concepts of consciousness and time, it was one of the last frontiers in terms of advancement. And at a time when every inked criminal in the northern hemisphere was sporting an inhibitor, there had never been a better moment to see if there were any sets of ink that could find their way through. It was probably a fool's errand. To be honest, he loved Julian just for trying. No matter what absurd heights the man had reached, he just kept reaching.

"This is bullsh—" the psychic nearly cursed in frustration, catching himself just in time.

Even if he complains every now and then.

"Try again," Devon said, twisting the coin between his fingers. "Take your time."

With a look of the utmost concentration, Julian closed his eyes and focused all his attention on the little trinket, his staggering mind stretching to the corners, trying to see if there was a way he could slip inside. There were a few moments when Devon thought he might have done it. His brow tightened and his head tilted to the side. But when he opened his eyes, they were stubbornly brown.

"I think it's impossible," he declared.

Devon grinned, sliding the coin secretly up his sleeve. "He says after a whole five minutes. Come on—try again."

There was a little sigh as the psychic straightened on the bench and set his mind to the task once more. He kept his eyes open this time, burning a hole in the space between them. After a few seconds, they flickered upwards—coming to rest on his friend.

"Don't read my face," the fox said chidingly, "read my future. Which hand?"

Julian tapped one at random. "That one."

Devon spat out the coin with a look of concern. "You really can't see? Not anything?"

"I can't even *begin* to see," the psychic answered, tugging petulantly at the chain around his neck. "It's like trying to climb a building, then realizing someone forgot to put in the stairs."

The door opened and Louis Keene paced across the mats, spotting them with the inhibitors and waving with a bright smile. "Good morning! How's it going with those things?"

The men shared a look.

"*Great!*"

"*Lots of progress!*"

He vanished through the doors, and they turned back to each other. Devon held the coin between them before hiding it deliberately behind his back.

"Find another set of stairs."

They continued working for the better part of an hour. Rather, the psychic continued working—grinding his teeth so hard, his jaw would ache the next morning—while the fox allowed his mind to wander, tossing the coin occasionally between his hands.

I missed this.

It wasn't just that he chafed at being trapped in some subterranean office, the weight of all that paperwork crushing him alive—he missed what was happening above ground. The chaos and the clamor. The bright flash of familiar faces, and happy voices echoing beneath the dome. He missed being able to measure a hard day's work by the strain in his muscles, not just his fingers. He missed being able to hang it all up at the end of the day, decisively closing the book.

Julian tapped him suddenly on the wrist. "Is it that one?"

He snapped back to the present, as the coin slipped from his fingers.

"Hmm?"

Julian picked it up with a teasing grin. "This is you helping?"

"Sorry," Devon murmured, hiding it once again. "I've just got a lot on my mind."

The psychic regarded him intently. "Tell me."

Where do I even begin?

"Well as you so eloquently put it, I've been dealing every day with the rise of some elusive shadow organization. Meanwhile, Kraigan's in a cave somewhere—bathing in the blood of the innocent. But if I'm being honest, it's Gabriel," he added unexpectedly. "I'm worried about him."

Julian glanced up in surprise. "How do you mean?"

An image of the assassin flashed through Devon's head—sitting at a crooked angle on the hallway floor, those piercing eyes blank and vacant, drifting aimlessly through the cloudy sky.

"He's just...pulling away from everything," he said quietly, remembering the frosty chill in the house. "You should have seen him on this mission the other day. There was this whole other side to him that just..." He shook his head. "He was like a different person."

Julian considered him a moment, then nodded thoughtfully. "Angel gets like that sometimes. Something will trigger a memory, and she'll get dragged back into it. I'll have trouble reaching her for a while." He leaned back on the bench, resting on his hands. "That metal we found in the museum? Cromfield was obsessed with the stuff. You should have heard Angel swearing about it on the phone. If there was ever something that was going to mess with Gabriel's head, I'm not surprised that's what did it."

Devon let out a sigh, twirling the coin in his hands. "Yeah, but Angel never—" He caught himself suddenly, jabbing a finger into the psychic's chest. "Speaking of Angel, she's being a holy terror! You need to stop playing around and divorce her already so we can move on with our lives."

He couldn't believe how many times he'd been forced to say it. He couldn't believe how many times the psychic had casually refused. *He'd fallen in love*, he'd always say. *Didn't the fox remember?*

Yes, he remembered Angel and Julian falling in love. He remembered with painful clarity. It was like watching your friend develop an arsenic addiction. Sooner or later, it was going to kill you.

"What has she done this time?" Julian asked, fighting back a grin.

Devon clenched his jaw. "She's trying to be friends," he replied stiffly.

There was a fleeting pause.

"Well, maybe she really—"

"This is like the time she claimed I was smuggling opium, so I'd be sexually assaulted by airline security," Devon said flatly. "This is like the time she bought me a new jacket in Uganda, but it was laced with that linseed oil to attract ants."

So. Many. Ants.

Julian went perfectly still, then flashed a charming smile. "I think I'm ready to try again with the coin."

Devon rolled his eyes and hid it behind his back.

They worked for a while longer, sitting in silence on the benches, while the rest of the agents went through their usual rotations. Climbing, and fencing, and wrestling, and hurling knives. The sky had darkened and it had started snowing again by the time they finally came to a stop.

"This is impossible," Julian complained, slumping back on the bench. "Of all the impossible things you guys make me try—this is the worst. It's like walking into an IKEA and asking one of *them* to tell the future. You're trying to make me do the supernatural without the use of my ink."

Devon offered a condescending smile. "Maybe if you were better—"

"That's nice." The psychic laughed. "You don't even know if this will work. If you're so confident, how about *you* give it a try?"

"Yours is so much easier to measure. How would I try?"

"I don't know," Julian answered, unlooping the chain from his neck. "Put it on, then try to jump really high."

The fox laughed in spite of himself, giving him a playful shove. "You make me sound like some kind of circus freak—"

"If the shoe fits."

They sat there a moment, smiling, but as the seconds ticked past, it faded from the fox's eyes. His friend was a balm, always had been. But he couldn't shake that nagging fear.

"Do you think we shouldn't do this tomorrow?" he asked quietly, studying the psychic for any clues. "Do you think I maybe shouldn't take Gabriel?"

Julian's eyes warmed with amusement. "I don't think people *take* Gabriel anywhere," he answered. "And do you really want to leave behind the only man who'd been there before?"

Devon regarded him intently. "What do you see happening?"

The psychic's eyes lit with an iridescent glow before darkening to brown.

"Not much," he admitted. "I can see you going there, now that you know where it is. But I can't see much of what happens inside. You haven't decided yet what you'll do. Either of you."

What is THAT supposed to mean?

"But do we find this metal?" Devon pressed. "Is it worth the trip?"

Julian slipped away again, for longer this time. The prophetic illumination brimmed past his eyes and swept over his skin—seeping like liquid starlight into his dark hair.

"You find...something," he said with a frown, trying to gather more. "The images keep shifting, there's too much left in the air. But it will be worth the trip. It moves things forward."

And I'M the circus freak.

Devon shook his head, muttering under his breath. "I should leave him behind."

"He'd only come along anyway," Julian replied. "And I can't believe for a second, he let anyone else see that address. If anyone's getting left behind tomorrow, it's you."

The fox huffed aloud, tilting his face to the ceiling. "Fine...you're right."

The psychic smirked. "I often am."

"Often, not always." Devon twirled the coin with a grin between them, before hiding it behind his back. "Guess which hand."

IT WAS DARK BY THE time Devon got home that night, a layer of fresh snow had blanketed the garden path. He parked carefully and stepped onto the pavement, only to see the silhouettes of two people sitting on the front porch. They were speaking quietly. Rather one was speaking—consoling, by the looks of it—while the other was nodding in miserable silence. After a moment had passed, the taller of the two lifted the other's chin, pressing a gentle kiss to their lips.

I should have circled the block.

"James?" he called loudly, crunching up the icy path.

They slid immediately away from one another, as he stepped out of the darkness and into the porch's light. His son looked vaguely irritated. His girlfriend had colored with a blush.

"Hey," James greeted him, rising for a one-armed hug. "I thought you and Uncle Gabriel were working late today."

"It is late," Devon replied a bit pointedly, glancing between them. "Are you guys turning in soon? I'd be happy to drive you home, Emma. The roads are pretty slick with ice."

She opened her mouth to reply, but James beat her to it.

"I can drive her home," he answered with a slight smile.

Don't be ridiculous. You're six years old.

"Of course," Devon said lightly. "I'll leave the light on for you." He headed into the house with a parting smile, but glanced back suddenly in the frame. "Gingerbread houses, right Jamie?"

Another teenager might have scoffed. But his son warmed with a lovely smile.

"I know," he replied. "I was just telling Emma."

Devon's own smiled faded a little as he dipped his head in the barest acknowledgement and stalked into the house. The lamps were still glowing upstairs, and the scent of freesias and lavender were drifting from the bathroom. He took off his shoes and padded inside, spotting a head of raven hair half-submerged in the tub. She glanced around when she heard him, brightening with a smile.

"It's cold out today. Did you see all that snow?"

"Yeah, I saw the snow." He perched on the edge of the tub, twirling his fingers in the fragrant steam. "You know that James and Emma are making out on the porch?"

She nodded, sinking further into the water. "They've been out there for a while." She dipped her chin into the bubbles, rising back out with a beard. "They're technically adults now, Dev. We need to start coming to terms with that. You know James says that Lily's started keeping a toothbrush at the palace?"

The fox glanced up with a frown. "Why does everyone keep mentioning that? That's such a strange thing to say."

"You don't get what he...?" She pursed her lips, like he'd done something adorable. "Never mind, sweetheart. The kids are twelve, and they'll always be twelve." She rolled her eyes. "I know you want to say they're eighteen and older, but they're twelve to me. You don't have to worry."

They're six.

"Don't pander," he said defensively. "Tell me what you mean."

She lifted halfway out of the water and took both his wrists, pulling him into the water with a mischievous grin. "Tell you what...how about I show you instead?"

Chapter 8

Gabriel flew up in bed with a gasp, pulse racing, skin prickling, sheets falling in a tangled pile around his waist. He sat there for a moment as the picture steadied, a hand clasped over his mouth.

He was lucky that his wife was away on assignment. It was nearly impossible to hide these moments when they were sleeping in the same bed. She would open her eyes just a second after he did—murmuring quiet comforts, stroking his hair. Sometimes, in the lull of her ministrations, he'd actually be able to fall back to sleep. Other times, he'd pace into the kitchen—standing directly beneath the bright lights. It scarcely mattered. It was a temporary salvation, nothing more. One way or another, the dreams would always find him. And he'd be back in those tunnels once again.

Enough.

He pushed swiftly from the bed, circling the room a few times, before flinging open the door and storming to the kitchen. It had been a while since he'd taken such measures, but he felt no shame in doing it now. The house was empty, and those bright lights were tempting.

He'd only stand there for a minute. Just long enough to catch his—

"Bad dream?"

He gasped again, flipping on the light switch to discover a handsome young man standing in the middle of the kitchen. He wore pajamas under a heavy winter coat, and his cheeks were pink with the cold. His blond hair was still flecked with an ivory dusting of newly-fallen snow.

"Jase?" he asked, as if to confirm it. "What are you doing here?"

The boy stepped forward, studying him just the same. "Alex called me," he answered casually, taking in all those little details, "said you'd had a nasty run-in with a tatù, said you probably shouldn't be alone." He paused a moment, noting the slight trembling in his father's hands. "You want to tell me what happened?"

Gabriel almost laughed aloud. How many times had such a thing happened in reverse?

When the boy had first come to him, he'd been wracked with nightmares—caught in their wicked thrall, unable to stop reliving the fire. Gabriel used to sit with him for hours, for weeks and years, asking that same quiet question, closing that tiny hand gently in his own.

But his son wasn't the only one plagued with nightmares.

When Gabriel had moved out of the tunnels and into his first apartment, that sort of thing used to happen all the time. The shakes, that was what Angel called it. The first few nights he'd woken up gasping, Devon had burst inside about four seconds later—hearing what his training could only interpret as 'the sounds of a struggle' from the other side of the street. Gabriel had cursed him and charged him for the broken window. But even his family had become accustomed to the dreams.

He remembered the first time a younger Jason had caught him in the kitchen—white-faced and trembling, standing with his face turned towards the lights. He'd jumped a mile when the child stepped into the room. Sometimes, he still forgot there was one living in the house.

"What are you doing?" the boy had asked.

A hundred excuses had leapt to Gabriel's tongue: he'd been training late in the Oratory, he was leaving early on assignment. He was changing the lightbulb. But the child had merely set about the same task he'd seen his new father do a hundred times before. He got him a glass of water.

Gabriel had sat at the table, watching as he crossed back and forth across the kitchen, trying to remember where everything was and assemble everything he would need for the simple task. He was tall for his age, but still only seven. In order to reach the glasses, he needed to grab a stepstool and drag it across the length of the room. Once there, he pulled down an empty mug and filled it to the brim—holding it with both hands, as he delivered it carefully to his father.

Gabriel remembered the pride on the boy's face when he presented it, the wet fingerprints smeared around the edges. He was a provider now, the water proved it. He repeated the question with a thoughtful frown, wearing an expression ten years older than he was.

"You want to tell me what happened?"

Gabriel startled back to the present, as an older voice repeated the same words. Jason was standing in front of him beneath the lights, an outstretched cup of water in his hands.

The assassin took it with a faint smile, shaking his head.

In almost twenty years, he'd never answered the question. He wasn't about to start now.

"You shouldn't be driving so late," he said instead, glancing out the darkened window, "not in this weather. Give me a second to find my keys, I can take you back to the flat."

Jason merely smiled, hopping onto the counter. "I heard you bailed Alexander out of jail," he said conversationally, swinging his legs just like he'd done as a boy. "I also heard you put him in charge of the transfers—that was clever."

Gabriel nodded briskly, tapping his fingers on the glass. "I am occasionally clever."

"Well, let's not get ahead of ourselves," the boy teased, eyeing him with a little smile. It was his father's smile, the one that painted neatly over everything happening underneath. "You're really not going to tell me what happened? Not the dream," he added quickly. His father never spoke of his dreams; he knew better than to ask. "The tatù. He said it was one of the transfers...?"

The smile took on the slightest edge, like someone had drawn a blade.

"Wouldn't tell me which one," he continued lightly, hopping off the counter. "The guy's convinced our family has anger issues. Something to do with you assaulting him in the school gym?"

Gabriel cracked a grin, dumping the rest of the water in the sink. "*Allegedly*, Jason. What do I keep telling you?"

"Allegedly," the boy repeated seriously. If there was one skill he'd picked up over the years, it was how to deliver such lines with a straight face. "I'm going to stitch that into a pillow."

The assassin laughed aloud, warming at the mere sight of him.

In the gaze of those blue eyes, it was suddenly easier to put things into perspective. He'd relived an old memory—nothing more. In the morning, he was going to an empty house.

"Devon and I are investigating one of Cromfield's storage facilities," he said unexpectedly, stunning the boy with his free use of the name. "It's got me a little spooked, that's all."

Better to be honest, it bred less questions.

"I've got some questions," Jason said tentatively.

Gabriel bowed his head with a sigh. "I don't have any answers, not tonight." He latched onto the sight of him once again, suddenly desperate not to be alone. "Are you staying? I could still drive you back."

Jason pulled a toothbrush from his pocket. "You up for a game of chess?"

THEY PLAYED UNTIL THE early hours of the morning, sipping hot apple cider and laughing in the glow of the fire. It was one of the first things they'd bonded over in the beginning—chess and sparring. To hear Gabriel talk about it, they were essentially the same thing.

They passed out in the living room around three in the morning, then rose with the sun at dawn. While his father got in the shower,

Jason flitted systematically through the house: turning on lights and latching windows, making sure the thermostat was working and the kitchen was stocked with food. By the time Gabriel swept down the hall, he was waiting with a mug of steaming coffee.

"Uncle Dev is pulling into the drive," he said quietly, pressing it into his hands.

The fox had already spotted them through the window—raising his hand in a little wave and flashing a quick smile. He'd been dreading the morning himself, but hadn't spent the night drinking cider and playing chess. He was pleased to see the lights back on, smoke rising from the chimney.

"Thanks," Gabriel murmured, taking a scalding sip of coffee and stuffing his arms into his coat. "This shouldn't take long. I'll be back in the evening if you'd like to—"

"Dad?"

Jason caught onto his sleeve, stopping that relentless momentum. For a moment, they just stared at each other. Nothing but the crackling hearth, the snowflakes whispering in the breeze.

"I could come with you," he said quietly, searching his father's eyes. "I could go for you. It's just a building to me, no history, no dreams. Just tell me what to look for—"

Gabriel extracted himself with a gentle smile, placing both hands on his son's cheeks. "I would rather set myself on fire than imagine you in that place. I'm going to be fine, Jase. I promise." He stared a moment, then kissed him suddenly on the forehead. "You're a good kid."

Jason smiled in return, unlatching the door. "I get it from Mom."

A moment later, the assassin was striding down the frosted walkway—making a mental note to have Rae melt a path when he returned home. He slid theatrically across the top of Devon's car, then yanked open the door—flinging himself into the passenger seat.

"We good?" the fox asked, eyeing him carefully.

He might have been idling on the curb, fiddling with the radio and staring at his hands, but he'd been able to hear every word that had been spoken inside the little house. When it came to the restless tempers that sometimes gripped the assassin, he'd learned to take cues from his son.

He worried when Jason worried. He smiled when he smiled.

Gabriel passed him the address. "Just drive."

Chapter 9

It was close. That was immediately unsettling.

Devon drove in a straight line for only ten minutes, past the same coffee shops and diners he frequented with his friends, until they turned onto a wide, shaded street in a residential pocket of London. It was one of the wealthier areas, the stately homes owned by diplomats, or generational money, or maybe even a member of the House of Lords.

He glanced around, then found the address and rolled to a stop alongside the curb. A tidy row of houses loomed on one side, a gated park stretched on another.

"This is fancy," he murmured, pocketing his keys. He peered up through the window at the ivy-covered walls, the neat fitted stone. "So it's an actual *house*," he added abruptly.

Gabriel kept his eyes on the dash. "What were you expecting?"

Not a house.

It was a term they used loosely—like *handler* and *spook*. Most of the safe houses he'd been to weren't houses at all. They were usually warehouses, or repurposed industrial facilities. Somewhere off the grid and unassuming. Somewhere away from the common world's prying eyes.

But this...? A ten million pound estate in central London?

This seemed more Cromfield's style.

He flashed a sideways look across the car, thinking again about Jason's quiet offer to go in his father's place. He imagined making the same offer himself. He imagined putting the keys back in the ignition and driving the other way. But he already knew how both those scenarios would end.

He would break my jaw. Then he would break my car.

"Shall we go inside?" he asked lightly.

Gabriel nodded, eyes still on the dash. "That's why we're here."

The words struck between them, but the assassin didn't move. His legs were braced against the door, his fingers curled around the chair. It looked like it would take a nova to pry him loose.

Or maybe a few simple words.

"Let's finish in there, then get back home," Devon said quietly.

Those green eyes flew to him, half-hidden behind a curl of golden hair. They fixed there with such intensity, the fox felt as though it would melt the skin right off his face. But whatever he was looking for, the assassin apparently found it. He nodded abruptly and got out of the car.

The air was shockingly cold, and their breath clouded—as they jogged together up the stone steps. The lock on the door was easy enough, a simple design no different from any other house on the street. Devon reached into his pocket, as though fumbling for keys, then pulled out a pick set instead. They had become a point of pride among the agents. His tatù gave him an unfair advantage; short of some catastrophe, he could pick a standard lock in two seconds flat. Granted, there usually *was* some catastrophe. But there wasn't that morning. The door sprang free at a touch.

They watched it crack open, shoulder to shoulder on the porch.

This was the part when they'd usually brace for a burst of gunfire. This was the part when Devon would hurl a percussion grenade, and Gabriel would call out a spiteful pun. But those halls were long since deserted, and there was no one left inside to answer such a barrage. They shared a silent look, and were about to step inside, when a sudden voice called out after all.

"Peter!"

They jumped in alarm, then looked around to an old woman who'd shuffled out of the house next door for her morning paper. She was waving with furious enthusiasm, beaming all the while.

"Peter!" she called again, waving even harder. "Look how big you've grown, I scarcely even recognized you! It's been the longest time!"

Devon stared in astonishment, then his eyes drifted to Gabriel.

Peter.

The assassin was frozen beside him, staring in a kind of daze. That famous composure had vanished, leaving him raw and bare. His lips parted to answer, but the words caught in his throat.

"How's your sister?" the woman continued, planting a hand on her hip. "She was always a spiteful little thing, but I bet she grew into a heartbreaker." She smiled again. "How's your dad?"

...oh dear.

At that point, Devon took matters into his own hands—giving the assassin a pointed nudge, as he waved brightly in return. "Look alive, Peter. The lady asked you a question."

Gabriel blinked and nodded, trying his best to rally.

"Fine," he said faintly. "Everyone's fine."

Truth be told, it was a rather poor performance. If the woman had pressed even a little bit harder, she could have poked it through with all sorts of holes. But she was old and hard of hearing, and the men didn't linger. The second he spoke, they waved again and stepped swiftly inside.

The moment the door swung shut, Devon stopped where he stood—ears pricked for any danger, eyes sweeping in a wide arc. There was nothing for him to find. Nothing and everything. It was a house, just like any other. All the same furniture, all the same rooms. Yet, it was a house that had frozen twenty years earlier. The place was a capsule, sealed tight as a tomb.

He took a step into the parlor, half-choking on the musty scent of stale air. The dust crept into his throat and coated his fingers. He wondered at the last time someone had been inside the building. How empty it was, how still. He imagined that Cromfield had purchased it outright, and no one had been coming there for years. There was no paper delivery service. No utilities to be paid.

This was Cromfield's safe house? Where are all the things he stored?

He looked around to Gabriel, wondering the best way to ask the question, but while the fox had lingered on the lower story, some instinct had made the assassin stride immediately past it, stirring up a cloud of dust as he came to a stop at the base of the wooden stairwell.

Devon following him quickly, standing at his shoulder.

"Do you remember any of this?" he asked.

Gabriel shook his head, but he started moving up the steps.

They came to a door on the second floor, bolted with a deadlock. The assassin lifted his hand automatically, but it fell just as swiftly to his side. "It's locked," he said simply.

It was something a child might say. Blunt and unassuming.

Devon glanced at the heavy bolt, thinking how easy it would be for the assassin to twitch his hand and snap the metal in half. He took it himself instead, wrestling with it for a moment, before his fingers pried the heavy bars apart. It fell with a clatter to the ground, landing in pieces.

"It's not locked anymore," he answered.

They drew a breath and stepped inside.

What the bloody...

Devon stepped inside and turned in a slow rotation, surprised at every turn. Surprised, and surprised again. If you had given him a week to describe the feel of that place, he could not have done it justice. He'd thought—given how it looked from the outside, given the condition of the lower levels—that it might continue to resemble a regular house. One with file cabinets and too many shelves. They would browse for a while, before finding the tambor, neatly labeled, in the back of a linen closet. The world would continue turning. They would shut the door and never look back.

But this was nothing like he'd expected. This was nothing like he'd ever seen.

It did look like a house, at least in build and design, but it was a house that had been rent in half: equal parts old Victorian and secret laboratory. Both styles spilled into each other, blending and overlapping in the strangest of ways. There was an antique sitting table, filled with glass beakers. A chaise lounge had been pushed in the corner, but the legs had sunk into a silver puddle and the cushion was stained with what looked like blood. Hot plates and dishrags littered the countertops, while leather-bound novels had been stacked along top of an empty aquarium in which something had most certainly died. Crates of strange-looking artifacts were mounted by the fireplace, the lace curtains had been starched and ironed and then scribbled with mathematical equations. Everywhere, there were papers. Everywhere there were files, and tape recordings, and handwritten notes.

Devon ventured inside a little farther, staring around with a grim sort of awe. It was hard to believe the place had once been functional. It was absurd beyond the point of reality—like a movie set someone had taken gleeful months to design. His eyes drifted curiously from one thing to the next, coming to land on a dilapidated toaster. Despite the clutter in the room, everything seemed to have a place. But the toaster was an anomaly, dented and thrust into a corner alone.

"What happened there?" he asked, glancing back at Gabriel.

He stopped immediately cold.

The assassin hadn't managed to step inside the room, he'd taken a single look and frozen at the door. One foot was still raised a few inches above the other, like the way had sealed over with glass. But it was his face that was the most striking. It was a face that Devon would never forget.

There had been a handful of occasions throughout the years, when the others had felt protective of Gabriel. Julian had mentioned it a few times. Rae had mentioned it more often than that. Angel had ripped a bomb from the wall and flown home at a casual phone call.

The fox had never understood it.

He'd never met anyone so capable, so unshakable. He'd never met anyone so instantly deserving of trust. There were some people who withered to ash when cast into a fire, and there were some people who defied the gods themselves and refused to get burned. Even when the man drove him crazy, even when he vowed to take his life—there wasn't a doubt in his mind that the assassin could handle anything the world decided to throw at him. He'd been raised beneath a cemetery, bottle-fed by Jonathon Cromfield. He'd infiltrated the Kerrigan Gang and lived to tell the tale.

He'd never understood why the others twisted their hands and whispered. He'd never understood their fretting or the quiet watchfulness in their eyes.

He understood it now.

Because that unshakable man—the one who could scale mountains, and break rocks, and bend the will of the people around him—that man was nowhere to be found.

He was just a child again. A child that had been taken before he was ready—cast into a world of locked doors and empty tunnels, before he had a chance to feel sunlight on his face.

This was a bad idea. I shouldn't have let him come.

"How about you wait downstairs," he said casually, glancing out the window like they ought to be more careful. "That woman outside was excited to see you. She might come to the door."

It was like a spell had broken. Gabriel's foot lowered to the floor.

"She's not coming to the door," he said softly, pacing inside. He paused in the middle of the floor, raising a quick look to the ceiling. "Let's just get what we came for and be done."

Devon nodded quickly, coming to his side.

It was a rare metal—one whose existence was known by only a handful of people on the planet. If you'd asked him that morning, he might have assumed it would stand out. But the house was stuffed to the brim with things of exactly the same caliber. He didn't know where to start.

"Can you sense it?" he asked hesitantly. "With your ink?"

Gabriel paused a moment, then shook his head. "There are too many things in here with metal. And there wasn't very much," he added unexpectedly. "Just a single slab of it. It kind of looked like...like armor."

Devon stared at the back of his head.

I should have brought Angel. I should have brought Julian.

"Okay, we'll start looking," he said lightly, glancing around. Usually, they'd split into pairs, but there was no way he was letting the assassin out of his sight. He didn't want to round a corner and find him lying prone somewhere, staring blankly into the shadows. "Let's start over here."

Together, the pair made their way through the house—drawing closer to examine certain things, trying hard not to look at others. No matter how many time he grasped for equilibrium, the fox found himself ceaselessly jarred by the strange combination of things. The bloody handkerchiefs piled in the microwave. The flower vase that had been filled with razors. He didn't know which was worse. The parts that were a laboratory, or the parts that were a house.

A little ways in, he came across a bedroom that was nearly empty, just a single mattress in the center of the floor. There was a stack of clothes in the corner—mostly for a girl, sized eight or nine. A brush was lying next to the window. Ivory hairs.

"Anything in there?" Gabriel asked, stepping up behind him.

"Nothing," he said quickly, closing the door. "Let's keep moving."

They searched through a few more rooms, keeping the talking to a minimum, before ending up in the bathroom. Given the item they were looking for, it was probably a lost cause—but they were trained intelligence officers and made a thorough sweep. Gabriel tapped strategic point in the wall, listening for anything hollow, while Devon opened the cabinet and took out a bottle of pills.

"What's this?" he asked, searching for a label.

The assassin plucked it from his hand, examining it for himself. "I never knew. Some kind of drug he used to give us."

Devon shot him a quick look. "Performance enhancers?"

"No, they just get you high. Help you sleep." Gabriel stared at them for a moment, fingers curling around the bottle. Then he passed it abruptly to Devon, sweeping out of the bathroom without a backwards glance. "Put that somewhere, will you?"

The fox waited until he was gone, then smashed the bottle in his hand.

They carried on a bit longer, opening drawers and checking closets, stumbling upon any number of ghastly things. A stack of missing persons photos with matching IDs. A leather strap to bite down upon, still marked with the tiny imprint of teeth. Bottles, upon bottles, upon bottles of cleanser. They were about to give up and call for backup, when Gabriel came to a sudden stop.

"That's it," he said, peering into an unlit room. "That's the tambor."

Devon ventured in cautiously, then knelt to examine it. For whatever reason, he'd been imagining another statue, even though he knew already that wasn't the case. It was a thin slab of metal, just like Gabriel had described—shaped almost like a breastplate, with a stain of blood along the side. On a whim, he slipped a hand beneath the corner and tried to lift it.

Not a chance.

"If this group is looking for tambor," Gabriel began, "this is all I know that's left. Those mines got blown up in an airstrike a few years ago." He combed a hand through his hair, unwilling to look at the piece straight on. "Not sure how we're going to get it out of here."

Devon pushed to his feet, wiping off his hands.

"Don't worry about that. A team will be here in the morning to catalogue everything. They'll bring something that can manage the weight. You don't ever have to see this place again."

There was a pause.

"What do you mean?" Gabriel asked.

Devon paused, caught off guard by his tone. "A team is coming to—"

"—to catalogue everything," the assassin interrupted. "I heard you. But then what?" He let the words hang for a moment before gesturing around the house. "You've seen the kinds of things he was working on in here. We should torch this place and be done."

"Torch it?" Devon repeated with a smile, as if he was joking. "Someone got the bug. We gave you a pass with the cathedral, Gabriel, but you can't set every place that offends you on fire."

The assassin flashed him a silent look. He'd been coddled by his wife, by his son. But the fox was like a straight arrow, moving relentlessly forward. There was no choice but to follow his path.

Unless you'd been down that path before.

"We should throw it away," he pressed quietly, circling around so they were standing face to face. "Look around you, this stuff is nothing but dangerous. It should never see the light of day."

"*Some* of it," Devon said carefully, keeping some space between them. "And *some* of it is cutting edge research. We can't just throw away hundreds of thousands of pounds of analysis and equipment. A lot of this stuff could be preventative—antidotes, vaccines, deterrents. We need to be rational, here. They're just things, Gabriel. They'll be used how *we* see fit."

"This is a mistake," the assassin murmured, shaking his head. He looked smaller the longer they stood in the house. Just six years old again, and the walls were caving in. "Devon...everything terrible I ever did came with a rational explanation. Can't we just..." He trailed away, pulse leaping with a spark of panic. "Can't we just think about this for a second?"

"*Hey.*" Devon put both hands on his shoulders, stepping deliberately into his line of sight. The conversation stalled and the panic suspended, as he stared deep into those green eyes. "Nothing bad is going to happen. Trust me."

Trust me.

Gabriel went utterly still, then took a step back.

He was out the door a second later, leaving the grisly place behind him without a backwards glance.

Devon stared after him in surprise, then hurried out to the stairwell himself—pausing to close drawers and cabinets as he went along. He paused before he left, glancing back at the old toaster against the wall. There was a dent in the corner. The perfect curve of a child's head.

He shuddered in silence, then slammed the door shut.

<hr />

DEVON FELT THE EXPLOSION before he heard it.

There was a vibration through the floorboards, too faint for most people to notice, but it made him sit bolt upright in bed. By the time he hurried to the window, a thick plume of smoke had already risen into the air. It was coming from the west, near the residential district. Too small to be a commercial fire, too big to have happened by mistake. He stood there in silence, the glow of distant flames reflecting in the frosted glass. A nameless dread stirred in his stomach, rising to his neck.

Please, don't be the same place.

He was out the door a second later, throwing a heavy jacket over his pajamas as he leapt into the car. It became clear after only a few minutes, he knew where he was going. Even if he wasn't just following the sirens, the roads had etched into his memory—having driven them so recently before.

He pulled up just as a third firetruck arrived on the scene, announcing itself in a manic burst of lights and sirens. The doors opened and a flood of ready people leapt onto the ground, only to pause almost immediately upon seeing the blazing inferno.

There was no need to hurry. There was nothing left to save.

"I knew it," Devon panted, stepping onto the sidewalk. Even standing so far away, he could feel the heat upon his face. "I bloody knew it."

A crowd had already begun to gather—people huddling in overcoats and slippers, gossiping as to what might have happened, who might have been inside. A fire in such a prominent location was sure to make the papers. The news trucks had already started to arrive.

"Ma'am?" a voice cut above the rest, scripted and perfunctory. "Ma'am I need you to take a breath and tell me what happened. Can you do that?"

Devon turned his head, glancing towards the house next door.

The woman he'd seen earlier was sitting outside on the steps—her shoulders wrapped in an unnecessary blanket, trying to give an account to a policeman, but coughing with every breath.

"I've told you once," she croaked, "I've told you a thousand times. My husband and I went to bed early after watching a round of *Jeopardy*. The man's hard of hearing, but he likes yelling at the screen. Anyway, we were fast asleep when all of a sudden, we heard this *bang*. It was louder than a freight train, I'm telling you. I've never heard such a sound in all my life."

The officer nodded patiently, a notepad poised in his hand. "And did you have any—"

"You know what's strange," she interrupted, "is that house has stood empty for years. It's a coveted neighborhood, let me tell you, it's been quiet as a grave. Then out of the blue, the boy who used to live there came back today. Lovely fellow, Peter. We used to share biscuits and tea."

The officer looked up slowly. Devon shrank back towards his car.

"Did you see Peter again tonight?" the man asked.

She shook her head obliviously. "No, I didn't."

You wouldn't. He would have made sure of that.

Her face twisted in sudden horror.

"You don't think..." She trailed off, unable to say it. "You don't think he was still inside when it...?" She leapt to her feet a second later, jabbing a frail finger into the air. "You need to get in there and look for him! Why is everyone just standing around?! You need to—"

"The blaze was directed inwards, ma'am." The officer took her by the shoulders, easing her gently back down. "That means it's too hot for us to go inside, and there won't be anything left in the wreckage. Lucky for you, though," he added without thinking. "Probably saved your house."

She wrenched herself free, bloodshot and glaring.

"*Lucky*?!" she repeated in a shriek. "You're going to sit here and tell me I'm *lucky*, when a young man just burned to death in that very—"

Devon walked away before she could finish. He'd heard enough.

FOR THE SECOND TIME that day, the fox broke into the assassin's house. This time, he didn't use a key. This time, he kicked the door right off its hinges.

"You blew it up, didn't you?!" he demanded, storming into the living room. "You went back to the safe house, and blew the thing up!"

Silence.

"Damnit, Alden!"

Gabriel was sitting beside a dwindling fire in his favorite recliner, staring in pensive silence at the flames. There was a bottle of whiskey on the table beside him, but he hadn't touched it. He'd flinched when the door flew into the hallway, but it wasn't enough to make him break his gaze.

"It was the wrong call," he said quietly. "I made a better one."

The wrong call?!

Devon picked up the bottle, hurling it into the flames. "I didn't say it on a whim, Gabriel!" he cried. "It's standard operating procedure! You're a President of the Privy Council! You enforce the rules, you don't break them! And given your general bias about the situation, you absolutely *don't* get to make those kinds of calls!"

The assassin met his gaze, fearless and calm. "What do I bring to this job, if not my experience?"

"What do you bring to this job?" Devon repeated. "You bring a steady hand, Alden. And for the first time I'm beginning to realize, you don't have the faintest idea what that is."

Gabriel pushed to his feet. "And you don't have the faintest idea what you're dealing with," he countered. "You talk about these things in hypotheticals, but I've actually *lived* it, Devon. The world would be a better place if we blew every one of those houses off the map. I'm not going to apologize for what I did."

"You should," Devon said curtly. "You should have grown up enough to be sorry. That stuff is already out there. The only thing you did by blowing it up, is cripple our side." He paced abruptly away from him, before circling back once more. "Why do you keep putting me in these situations? Why do you keep forcing me to give the same lectures I give my kids? You cannot blow things up because you feel like it, Gabriel! This is Burundi all over again!"

"This is nothing like Burundi!" the assassin shouted, finally losing his temper. "This is Jonathon Cromfield, and there isn't a person on the planet who knows more about that than me!"

The words struck like thunder, shaking each man to the bone. They'd thought they were building bridges, but it was nothing but tinder between them. Dry kindling, just waiting for a spark.

Gabriel stepped even closer, eyes brimming with rage. "I lived through that terror once, I'm not going to stand around and watch as you zip his experiments into little bags, and the process starts all over again. This ends *here*! It ends with *me*!"

The smell of burnt whiskey drifted into the air. Pieces of broken glass glittered amongst the flames. For what felt like the span of a lifetime, Devon held his gaze.

Then he took a step back.

"It's too late for that," he said quietly, shaking his head.

Gabriel tensed in front of him, still primed for battle. "What do you mean?"

He'd expected more shouting. He'd probably expected them to come to blows. But all the fight had drained out of his opponent. The fox merely stood in front of him, staring back in a daze.

"I gave the order this afternoon," he breathed, arms hanging limp at his sides. "The council signed off and commissioned an evidence recovery team. It's already on the books, Gabriel. They've already given it a case number and a file."

He paused for a moment, unable to believe what was coming next.

"I have to report you."

A FULL DAY PASSED. Then another.

Devon locked himself in his home office and pretended to work. There were a few tentative knocks on the door, but he ignored them. He shuttered the windows, turned off his phone. He'd like to have said he went in there with some kind of plan. He was a man borne of plans, it unsettled him to flounder. Maybe he'd hoped some answer would reveal itself. Or maybe Carter would decide to come back after all and take the impossible decision off his hands. But Carter wasn't coming, and he was running out of reasons to stall. No matter which way he parsed it—and he'd sliced it down to the quick—he couldn't find a way out of the situation.

This wasn't a favor he could grant. A mistake he could pretend hadn't happened. He was a President of the Privy Council and his friend had broken one of their most basic laws.

I shouldn't have given the order, he thought desperately, pacing endless hours in front of his window. A light was shining in the house across the street. *I shouldn't have commissioned the team.*

At the time, he hadn't thought twice about it. If anything, Gabriel would be grateful the logistics were handled and he wouldn't need to spend any more time thinking about the place himself. It had been madness—what the assassin was suggesting. Set the building on fire and walk away? Even as he'd said it, even as Devon saw the spark of panic in his eyes, he couldn't believe the assassin himself was taking it seriously. It was an impulse, nothing more. The way a person paused before stepping into the street, or retracted their hand from a lit stove. These things could hurt you.

But there was use in them as well.

I should have taken him somewhere different, made him talk it out. We could have spent the night wandering the city, gotten it all out of his system—

But even as Devon thought the words, a simmering anger kindled back to life.

Why should he have taken extra precautions, treating the man who was supposed to be his partner like a child? Why should he have anticipated that instead of following basic procedure, his friend would decide to sneak back in the dead of night and set fire to the building instead?

For all he knew, there were things inside that shouldn't burn. Powders, explosives. Old crates of munitions that Angel kept alongside her hairbrush. And what of the tambor? What if something like that *couldn't* burn? It would be discovered in the wreckage, gleaming and undamaged, a gift to the highest bidder—to be twisted and contorted in all sorts of unpredictable ways.

He'd started out angry when he'd stormed back to the house. He'd slammed the door of his office hard enough to make the pictures and diplomas clatter off the wall. As the days passed, he'd grown thoughtful, then scheming. Then desperate. Now, he was angry once again.

This isn't my problem. Gabriel did this—reckless and without consideration. And at some point, Gabriel is going to have to take responsibility for his actions.

In a burst of vindictive decisiveness, he threw open and door and stormed down the stairs, ready to fling his frustration and temper at the first person who happened into his path.

He came across his wife, reading in the living room.

Not ideal, but okay.

"He emerges," she said placidly, lowering the newspaper a few inches to study him over the top. "Are you ready to talk about it? Or would you like to spend a few more days locked like a bat inside your office?" She eyed him speculatively. "You have to be nearly out of clean clothes."

It wasn't the resistance he'd been hoping for, but he pushed against it nonetheless.

"Gabriel blew up the Cromfield safe house," he announced, unfurling the truth before her. "I told him we needed to take it back to headquarters as evidence, and he went back anyway and blew it up."

He'd expected a gasp, a profanity. A pale reflection of the indignant fury that had been keeping him awake for the last two nights.

She pursed her lips, folding up the paper. "Yeah, I figured."

He floundered before her, like a ship that had lost its sails. "...you did?"

"Well, I saw the fire from our bedroom window," she explained, pushing to her feet. "I've also been hearing you rage about it for the better part of the weekend." She crossed the space between them on slippered feet, winding her arms around his waist. "So it's pretty bad, huh?"

He let out a tired sigh, wilting against her. "He acted against the council's orders, Rae. I have to report him."

She stared up at him calmly, the fire glowing on her face. "There have been plenty of times we've acted against the council's orders."

"But that was different," he argued wearily. "Half the time, we'd already separated from the agency. And the other times, Carter had sanctioned our missions in secret behind their back. And that was always for some higher cause," he added, running a hand through tangled hair. "We were racing to save hybrids from Cromfield, or battling ideologies with Mallins. It was never something like this. A personal grievance. A childhood trauma that could only be silenced in flames. We have rules for a reason," he concluded, repeating the same words he'd been chanting to himself. "For better or worse, they hold things together. We can't just decide that some of them don't count."

She pressed a kiss to his collarbone, squeezing her arms around his ribs. "I know you think the rules are important," she murmured. "And for all his nonsense, I know that Gabriel thinks so too. Maybe even more than the rest of us. You're acting like he rushed over there on some rash vengeance, but that isn't Gabriel. He doesn't do things without considering all the angles. I guarantee he thought about all of this before he lit the fuse."

Devon pulled back a few inches, looking down in surprise. "Do you agree with him? Are you saying he was right to blow it up?"

"No, I don't think he should have. I'm just saying, this might not be as black and white as you think." She paused a moment, regarding him intently. "You said that you have to report him, but you haven't yet. It's been two days. What's holding you back?"

I don't want him to get in trouble. I don't want him to lose his job. I don't want to take a battering ram to all the progress he's been making, and put a man who's nothing short of miraculous back on the street.

"I don't know," he mumbled. "Lots of things."

There was a knock on the door.

"To be continued..." Her eyes twinkled as she tightened the belt on her robe, heading off the answer it. "Don't go anywhere, Wardell. The second we finish down here, I'm going to force you into the shower. Then I'm going to force you into bed."

He smiled in spite of himself, something he wouldn't have thought possible just a few minutes before. The newspaper was still folded on the coffee table where she'd left it; a familiar picture splashed across the front. He leaned down to examine it.

"Is that St. Stephen's?" he asked curiously. "I thought it got demoted to a gym."

She shook her head, padding down the hallway. "They reconstructed the original cathedral. It's re-opening tomorrow." She cast a glance over her shoulder. "When it rains, it pours huh?"

Yeah, I guess.

He stared down at the picture, tracing over the gothic spires. It was a lovely building, no denying that. When he was little, his mother used to take him there on special occasions—Easter and Christmas. He'd kicked his legs against the pew, waiting impatiently for a pastel bunny to leap from the rafters. Of course, it was impossible not to go back and reexamine things. While he'd been sitting in the sunlight, dreaming of chocolate, his friend had been just a few feet below—wandering aimlessly through the shadowy tunnels, listening to faint strains of music come down from above.

He let out a breath, remembering the look on Gabriel's face when that door had swung open. The quiet, blinding terror that had rooted him to the spot. Maybe his wife was right. Maybe absolutes were tales for children, and they were all just living in the gray.

"Devon," Rae called softly from the foyer, "there's someone here to see you."

He lifted his head, then walked briskly down the hallway to join her. It was late, too late for visitors, and there were only a handful of people it might be. Still, it wasn't who he was expecting.

"Natasha," he greeted her in surprise.

The girl was standing in the doorway, wrapped in a thick overcoat that belonged to her husband, dripping a steady puddle of water onto the floor. Her eyes were red, but she hadn't been crying. If anything, it looked like she'd been pacing for two days just the same as him.

"Hi, sorry to come by so late." She cast a quick look at Rae, still hovering in the doorway beside her, and gave her hand a little squeeze. "Can I steal him for a minute?"

"For as long as you like," Rae answered warmly, squeezing her in return. She tapped a finger on Devon's nose as she walked past. "Straight to the shower, then straight to bed."

He shook his head with a faint grin. "Yes, ma'am."

The two stood in awkward silence until she'd vanished up the stairs—making a point to shut the door behind her. When at last they were alone, that silence only got heavier. It pulsed like a living thing between them, freezing them like reluctant statues and catching in their throats.

Say something. You know why she's here.

"It was already on the books, Natasha. There was already a whole team of people who—"

"I'm not here to talk about that," she said quickly, taking off her hood. Her honey-tinted hair glistened with raindrops, twisted into a delicate knot on top of her head. It had been years since she'd quit dancing, but the lovely ballerina still carried herself with a breathless grace. "I wanted to show you something, if that's all right...?"

It took Devon a moment to understand what she was saying. When it finally clicked, his pulse quickened. His eyes flickered without permission to her hands.

"Right now?" he asked nervously. "I mean...sure, alright."

A touch of humor stirred in her eyes, as she took a step closer. Of all the people who'd experienced the sudden burst of her tatù, Devon had undoubtedly liked it the least. It was cerebral enough that he chafed against it being a shared activity. It was an utterly foreign sensation, the feeling of someone else in his mind. Julian liked it so much, he'd been temporarily banned.

She reached out both hands, placing them lightly on the sides of his face.

"Take a breath," she instructed.

By the time he complied, the bright lights of the foyer had already vanished and the world as he knew it was gone. They were somewhere different now, somewhere darker—damp without revealing the source of it, with a chill that seeped through his clothing and into his very bones.

We're underground, he realized. *But this isn't...this can't be her mind.*

The faint strains of an organ drifted from above.

Devon's breath caught, and he went perfectly still.

More times than he cared to admit, he had imagined what it must have been like in those tunnels—now he saw the truth firsthand. His mind had sparked with a thousand horrors—blades and scalpels rusted with blood, skeletons mounted up for study. Long tables fitted with manacles, as the screams and wails of the innocent pierced through the lightless air.

The screams were real enough, but they were rare and faded to the background. As for the rest of it, it closer resembled a tomb. There was just...nothing. No colors, no sounds. No people, no lights. Just a single, unending tunnel that seemed to stretch through the very center of the ear.

There was a quiet sound behind him, enough to make him jump. He whirled around in a daze, scarcely aware of Natasha standing beside him, then froze in horror at what he saw.

A little boy was playing in the darkness, golden curls spilling forward, his cheeks stained with the tracks of old tears. He wiped at them without thinking, hopping from one stone to the next. A man cried out in the distance, but he scarcely noticed. His green eyes were fixed upon his game.

Gabriel.

Devon clasped a hand over his mouth, unaware that he'd begun to cry.

The cave was freezing, but the child was barefoot. Something on him was bleeding. Had he been punished? Some accident he inflicted on himself? Never had he felt more like a father. He wanted to scream, to throw up, to shake the world on its axis. He wanted to gather the child in his arms and sprint in the opposite direction—give him a jacket, give him a home.

How could such a thing have been allowed to happen? How could such a beautiful little spirit have been trapped in such horror all alone? But he wasn't alone, that was the problem.

A voice drifted out of the dark.

"*Gabriel.*"

The boy lifted his head immediately, like a puppy hearing his master's call. Like flipping a switch, what little color there was drained from his cheeks, leaving him ghost-white and trembling.

Run! Devon almost screamed aloud. *Run!*

But Gabriel didn't run. The instinct to run had been beaten out of him. Along with any hope there was something better waiting on the other side. He stilled for only a moment, his eyes staring into the shadows. Then he took off at sprint, vanishing into whatever darkness lay beyond.

The image cleared slowly, warming into focus in the glow from the lights.

Devon took a step for balance, letting out a fractured gasp. The cave was gone, but his head was still spinning with it. A splintering ache had started deep in his chest.

A crazed part of him wished he could go back. That he could rescue that boy from the hell that had ensnared him, drag him from the shadows into the sun's warm light. Another part couldn't bear thought. Another part felt like if he stayed in that cave a second longer, he would go mad.

Natasha put a hand on his arm, keeping him steady.

"For years, that was his entire life," she said quietly. "For *years*. No one ever knew. No one ever came to save him." She paused moment. "All of it was done in the name of the greater good."

It was quiet a few seconds, then she hopped onto her toes and kissed his cheek. "Goodnight."

"Goodnight," he echoed faintly as she slipped through the door.

He stood in silence after she left, staring unblinkingly at the wall. The minutes slipped past, one after another. Then he reached into his pocket, and pulled out his phone.

Chapter 10

Gabriel sat in the school parking lot, staring unflinchingly through the windscreen.

He had made up his mind the night before—sometime between picking bits of broken glass from the fireplace, and wondering what had happened to his wife. It had been a snap decision, the kind of thing that was easy to quantify when he was steeling himself up in the bathroom mirror.

Now that the moment was upon him, he was having trouble getting out of the car.

Just do it, he commanded himself. *Walk inside and tell them what you've done.*

As the fates would have it, the timing couldn't have been better. It was the third Friday of the month—the council's regularly scheduled staff meeting. They usually spent the time bickering over case assignments, or plotting governmental rebellions. There were usually doughnuts in the center of the table, and someone would spontaneously turn into a bear. They were usually a decent amount of fun, but it wouldn't be this morning. This morning, Gabriel would have his last one.

Don't be a coward, open the door.

He let out a quiet breath, resenting the inherent ease of the voice inside his head. It preached a world where things were so simple. Go inside, confess to a weighty crime, and pray that all those friendly faces won't put down their doughnuts and drag you off in chains. *Imprisonment*. It was an option he hadn't thought of until driving to the school.

The sudden jolt of it had almost made him turn right back around. No, he didn't think they would lock him up. Not for something like this.

But they would strip him of his title—that they would *have* to do. They would take him off the field rotation, suspend his international privileges. If he was being honest, there was a half-decent chance they would fire him. But he couldn't think about that option right now.

Not if he ever wanted to get out of the damn car.

You've already decided to do it. What are you waiting for?

A miracle, a comet. Some flash of supernatural magnificence that would erase everything that had happened in the last three days and let him start anew. It was probably a much simpler solution. He probably should have just asked Rae to go back in time.

Because there was another reason he didn't want to step inside that staff meeting, there was another thing he'd realized while scrubbing scorching whiskey out of his fire.

He might have been wrong.

Even the hypothetical was enough to send his heart racing, but no matter how many times he tried to assure himself that couldn't possibly be the case, the more that nagging voice started whispering in his ear. Not Devon's voice—that one had been silenced. It was his own words that haunted him. His own nagging doubts.

There were good people inside that building, trying to cheerfully kill each other beneath the massive dome. People who made good decisions, people who brought doughnuts. There was a chance he should have trusted those people with something like this.

Not everyone was Jonathon Cromfield. Not every punishment was an agony, not every conversation ended in blood. If he wanted to get on with his new life, he'd have to stop living in his old one. Devon was right. It *killed* him to say it, but Devon was right.

Sooner or later, everyone has to grow up.

Carter's going to be so disappointed.

He bowed his head with another sigh, then pushed open and door and stepped onto the wet pavement. It had rained in the night, melting whatever remained of the winter snow. His boots slid the second they made contact, and he nearly collided with the exact person he needed to see.

Coincidentally, it was also the last person on his list.

"Hey," he gasped, catching Devon's arms for balance. "Sorry, I didn't see you."

The fox went dead still the moment they locked eyes, staring back with the strangest look Gabriel had ever seen. A little spasm went through his shoulders, and he reached compulsively forward—almost like he was considering giving the assassin an embrace.

He probably wants to punch me instead.

"I'm sorry," Gabriel said again, more directly. "You were right. I shouldn't have blown up that safe house. Whatever happens next, I take full responsibility."

If he'd lit himself on fire, Devon couldn't have looked more surprised.

"...you do?"

The assassin nodded curtly, wishing it was already done. "It was a mistake. I was afraid if I left it..." He trailed off, shaking his head. It didn't matter anymore. "I don't know why you haven't already told them, but I'm going to do it right now."

As if on cue, the doors of the Oratory opened and a group of people started drifting towards them across the lawn. They were chattering away, breath clouding in front of them, as they made their way to the cars. Devon cast a quick look over his shoulder, as Gabriel stared with a little frown.

"Isn't that Keene?" he asked in confusion, recognizing the man's dark coat. "Why are they leaving already? We haven't even..." He trailed off, staring at Devon's face. "You moved up the meeting," he said in understanding. "You already told them."

It was a smart move—doing it when Gabriel wasn't there. To be honest, it was probably a kindness. His eyes strayed over the fox's shoulder, as his pulse quickened with a thrill of dread.

"Okay," he said, trying to steady himself. "So what should I—"

"Nice work, Alden!"

He lifted his head as a voice called out from the crowd. They were closer now, just a stone's throw away. Before he could formulate a response, they had already joined them.

"Tough break with the power lines, but what can you do?" Keene continued, clapping him on the shoulder. "We'll get it next time."

The others flooded past them, offering similar words of condolence, before filtering off in separate directions and getting into their cars. There was a sound of roaring engines, a dozen bursts of steam, as one by one, they made their way out of the lot.

Gabriel stared until the last one vanished, before turning to Devon in shock.

What the heck?

"The storm knocked over a utility pole last night," the fox explained, "collapsed it right on top of our safe house. The power line caught fire...burned the whole thing to a crisp."

There was a beat of silence.

"Power lines," Gabriel repeated, unable to believe it was true.

"That's what it says in the official report," Devon answered, opening the door to his car. He glanced back at the last moment, offering the ghost of a smile. "Really tricky, those things."

The assassin let out a breath, watching as he sped out of the lot.

They certainly are.

⁂

IN LIEU OF HIS SCHEDULED tragedy, Gabriel got back in his car and turned onto the interstate, speeding his way to the foggy streets of London. No matter how much time passed, he couldn't wrap his head around it. He kept waiting for the alarm to sound, waking him from a dream.

Natasha was already up by the time he got home, listening to music and hanging things up in the closet. He slipped inside without her noticing, wrapping his arms around her waist.

"Freeze," he whispered, kissing her cheek.

She whirled around with a screech, kicking him in the shins. "...Gabriel?"

"That was really good, love!" He kissed her again, unable to keep the creeping smile off his face. "If that had been a real intruder, you'd *definitely* have given him a bruise."

She smacked him with a grin. "You bet I would have."

His eyes strayed past her, towards the open closet. "Did you wear my coat?"

"Gabriel," she summoned back his attention, waiting impatiently. "How did it go?"

There was an agonizing silence, then he smiled.

"There was a big storm last night," he replied, lifting a shoulder like it couldn't have been more casual. "Knocked over a utility pole and set the safe house on fire."

...with a handful of trinitrotoluene explosives.

She beamed in return, biting down on her lip. "Bad luck," she murmured.

"Indeed."

They stood there for a moment, then he scooped her up with a joyous *whoop*, spinning her around and around. The relief was almost dizzying, like a giant stone had been lifted from his chest.

Not just because he'd escaped the consequences of his little pyrotechnics, but because if he ever found himself in the same situation—he didn't think he'd make the same choice again.

Progress. Sometimes it hits you like a storm.

"Do you want to grab a bite to eat?" he asked excitedly, setting her back on the floor. "I could call up Jason, see if he and Aria want to—"

"I have a better idea," she interrupted, taking him by the wrist. "How about a picnic in bed?"

THREE HOURS LATER, the picnic had yet to materialize. The happy couple had yet to notice its absence, they'd found other ways to fill their time instead.

"Show me that move again?" Gabriel stretched out across the full length of the bed, gazing up adoringly at his stunning wife. "The fous…the foust…?"

"The fouette?" she corrected with a grin, stretching a leg up behind her. "It's meant to be done while spinning, Gabriel. Not on a bed—"

"How very unimaginative," he interrupted, pulling her towards him. Their limbs tangled as they came together, sharing a lingering kiss. "Now, I know you said you were hungry," he began, trailing his fingers down her sides, "but what if I could convince you—"

There was a sudden vibration on the nightstand.

He dropped his head onto the pillow with a breathtaking profanity, then groped blindly for his phone—tilting the screen so he could see who was calling.

"Sheesh—it's Devon."

"Ignore it," she instructed, trailing kisses down his chest. "You ignore the call, and I'll pretend I'm not still hungry."

He chuckled, reaching for it anyway. "Can't ignore it. He might have changed his mind." He propped himself on the pillows, trying to switch gears. "Hey, Dev. What's up?"

The fox's voice echoed through the line. "Want to come over?"

Gabriel glanced down with a grin as she raked her teeth across his stomach. "Not really."

A second later, her own phone buzzed with an incoming text. She took a second to read it, then hopped cheerfully off the bed. "I'm going out, love. Angel's taking me to the shooting range."

Gabriel stared after her, then lifted the phone. "Scratch that. I'll be there in five."

⁜

EXACTLY FIVE MINUTES later, Gabriel was standing on the Wardells' front porch.

It was a lovely winter's morning, and not just because he'd recently escaped the threat of unemployment or possibly even jail. The sun had made a rare appearance, and the thick fog that had enveloped the city at sunrise had already burned away. He knocked four times, admiring the view.

The door opened a second later, and Devon appeared in the frame.

"You knocked," he said in surprise.

"You perjured yourself," Gabriel answered with a smile.

They stared at each other a moment, then the fox beckoned him through the door.

Since Aria had moved down to the river with Jason, there had been decidedly less chaos in the house at the end of the street. That being said, the girl wasn't made in a vacuum. The assassin stepped carefully into the foyer, staring at the live oak tree that was growing at the base of the stairs.

"You guys redecorating?" he asked lightly.

Devon glanced over his shoulder, like he'd already forgotten. "Oh, right." He rolled his eyes, waving Gabriel towards the kitchen. "It's Jamie's revenge. Apparently, we're going to have spring break right here. He threatened to add fish."

No water. Just fish.

The assassin chuckled under his breath, following him inside.

Despite how casual they'd grown over the years, there wasn't often a reason that one of the men would call the other for the mere pleasure of their company. They'd spent more time together than either could count, but it was usually in the presence of one of the others—a buffer, for when their jokes got a little too sharp, and their smiles took on an edge.

Gabriel kept waiting for the reason of today's visit to reveal itself, but the fox merely stood in the middle of the kitchen. After a few seconds, he broke the silence himself.

"So what's it going to be, Wardell? You want me to thank you properly?"

Devon drew in a breath, deciding never to ask what that might mean. "It's Rae and my anniversary," he announced.

Gabriel nodded, then frowned. "That can't be right."

"It's the anniversary of the first time we went skiing," Devon explained, flushing when the assassin raised his eyebrows. "Amongst other things. She's big on anniversaries."

Apparently.

"So what?" Gabriel asked. "You want some pointers, or—"

"Natasha says you know how to cook."

For the first time, Gabriel's eyes flitted over the kitchen—a normally immaculate place that now looked like a small agrarian bomb had exploded right in the center. They circled around the haphazard piles of produce before returning to the man standing in the middle.

"She says you're a *great* cook," Devon added with a coaxing smile. "I was hoping maybe you could help me make dinner?"

There was a pause.

"On your anniversary? For your wife?"

Another pause.

"We don't have to do it naked or anything."

Gabriel sighed and rolled up his sleeves. "Why not."

Twenty minutes later, he was rethinking that notion.

They had started by going to the store. Devon had purchased a small truckload of produce already, but was somehow still missing one or two key ingredients. Once they were inside, it was like trying to contain a kid in a toy shop. The fox kept racing up and down the aisles, filling the cart with a mismatched assortment of things, changing the recipe a million times to *things Rae might like better.*

When they finally got home, the real trouble began.

"How is it possible you've never done this before?" Gabriel asked incredulously, watching as his infallible friend struggled to grate cheese. "How have you survived?"

Devon kept his eyes on the task, panting slightly. "God invented this thing called take-out..."

"I would have pegged you for a fitness nut," the assassin continued. "Lecturing the rest of us on the critical importance of eating three square meals a day."

"That's not true," the fox said defensively, tying back his hair. "I know for a fact that Angel can survive on nothing but breath mints and cardboard."

The gods made her different.

It didn't help that Devon had settled on a strange recipe for jambalaya—something that required a hundred ingredients and needed to simmer for hours on the stove. By the time they were finished, Rae would have gone on to create needless anniversaries with someone else.

It also didn't help that he required *constant* instruction.

"What now?" he asked, bouncing from foot to foot.

Gabriel sighed, glancing down at the laptop. "Add the celery," he answered. "Wash it first." The fox rinsed it thoroughly in the sink, then glanced expectantly over his shoulder. The assassin prayed for patience, speaking the way one might address a small child. "Now put it on the chopping block."

"Chopping block, right."

Devon glanced helplessly in both directions, biting at his lip, until Gabriel paced forward and pulled it from the counter. The fox's mouth fell open in astonishment.

"That's been here the whole time?"

Seriously, kill me now.

"Now chop it up," Gabriel instructed, rifling in the refrigerator for another beer. "Not that one,"—he peeled one off and tossed it in the trash—"that one's bad."

The fox went perfectly still. "How do you know?"

"Because it was brown, the others were green."

"...what about the rest of it?"

"It's fine, Dev. Don't worry about it."

"But—"

"Chop the celery."

There was a pause.

"It says to *dice* it," Devon countered apologetically, glancing at the screen. He hesitated a moment, frowning in concern. "Is that different?"

"Here." Gabriel took the knife, cutting it into strips. "It's like when you break someone's wrist," he explained. "You see the motion?"

Devon nodded and took over, smiling to himself all the while. "Look," he said proudly when he was finished, "just like in a restaurant."

Gabriel gave him a long stare, then opened up the beer. "Yeah. Just like in a restaurant."

At a painstaking speed, they made their way through the rest of the ingredients—one of them drinking heavily, while the other questioned every turn. Devon seized enthusiastically upon what he termed 'knife-work,' then had a crisis of confidence when he got to the spices.

"I bought a little bit of everything..." he said sheepishly.

Gabriel pursed his lips. "I can see that." He pointed to the recipe on the screen. "It says a tablespoon. You know which one that is?"

Things like pride and dignity had been abandoned long ago. Without a breath of hesitation, Devon held out a cluster of tiny spoons, watching as the assassin selected the right one.

"That much paprika?" he asked.

"You can do a little less," Gabriel replied. "I usually do. I'm not wild about the taste."

The fox looked up with a start. The Privy Council had bred perfection, and he didn't like things with guesswork involved. "But it says..." He trailed off, looking at the spoons. "Look, we're not going to make this one of those *things*, alright? We're going to do what the computer tells us."

Gabriel raised his eyebrows dangerously, leaning back against the counter. "One of *what* things?"

"You know what things."

"I think you should tell me...*right now*."

Devon stared at him, then carefully measured out the precise amount listed online. "The next one's a teaspoon," he said mildly, holding out the cluster.

Gabriel handed back the right one.

"Now the pepper you want to be careful with," he said, as an extra dollop poured over the side. "Do a little bit less in the next one since you went over."

There was a buzz in his pocket.

Thank the gods.

He pulled out his phone, smiling as a name flashed up on the screen. "How's it going, love?"

"Gabriel?" A barrage of sound echoed through the line as his wife shouted straight into the receiver. "Gabriel—I hit the target!"

There was a tapping on his shoulder.

"That's wonderful, sweetheart!"

"The other guy's target," Angel muttered in the background.

More tapping.

He turned his back, covering his other ear.

"You two about finishing up?"

Please, say yes.

"I could stay here for ages!" she cried.

His eyes snapped shut. "That's great."

More tapping.

He finally turned around to see Devon standing beside him, demonstrating what 'a little bit less' might look like in the teaspoon. He stared with saucer-eyes, waiting for approval.

Gabriel gave him a drawn out look, then flashed a sarcastic thumbs up.

Unbelievable.

Natasha kept chattering obliviously, while Angel fired off rounds from a semi-automatic in the background. But by far the most dangerous situation was brewing right there at home. Gabriel watched as Devon dumped the pepper into the pot, then waited impatiently for the next spices, twirling the cutting knife at such impossible speeds, he was bound to lose a finger.

"Hang on, babe." Gabriel covered the phone. "You can go on and do the rest of them."

Devon's eyes widened ever so slightly as they lifted to the recipe, before he shook his head with a little smile, frightened of his own daring. "I'll wait."

Fantastic.

On and on it went.

After getting over the initial fear response, Devon seemed to enjoy adding in the spices, peering down like some mad scientist as he stirred them frantically, lifting the spoon to the light as he measured out precise amounts. When they finally reached the end and Gabriel went to add the broth, he seized the cup from his hand with supernatural speed.

"Let me do it."

He poured it in slowly, smiling to himself as the colors began to blend. Gabriel took a single look and thought of all the ways he might kill him. He grabbed another beer instead.

"There," he declared. "It's done. You just let it simmer for the next four hours."

The fox stared back incredulously, unable to believe it was true. "We just...walk away?" he asked.

"We just walk away."

It should have been the easiest instruction of them all, but for whatever reason, the fox was clearly incapable of doing it.

Gabriel set down his beer with a sigh. "Do you want to stir it first?"

Devon lit up. "Yeah, maybe a few times..."

THERE'S TOO MUCH FOOD. *Come for dinner.*

That was the text Gabriel got a few hours later.

He stared at it for a full ten minutes, before letting out a slightly hysterical laugh, grabbing Natasha's hand, and dragging her down the sidewalk to the cottage at the end of the street.

They weren't the only ones who'd received a summons. Molly and Luke were already setting up chairs in the backyard, while Julian had been tasked with lecturing James on the colorful array of woodland vegetation that had been springing up all over the house. A picnic in the middle of winter might have seemed like a foolish notion, but with a little supernatural intervention, the Wardell's backyard was a good twenty degrees warmer than the rest of the city. Even now, Rae was walking in careful circles around the garden, leaving a trail of muddy water behind her feet.

Natasha watched them for a moment, then leaned over with a grin. "These remain the strangest people I'm ever going to meet."

Gabriel snorted under his breath. "You have no idea..."

As she wandered over to help Molly, he made a beeline for Rae—catching her attention just as she was attempting to resurrect a potted Ficus that had withered in the garden.

"Happy anniversary," he declared.

She flashed him a strange look, dusting off her hands. "What?"

"Devon said it was your anniversary," he replied with a touch of confusion. "The first time you guys ever drove across a toll bridge or something. He told me this, after basically abducting me to help him cook this little feast," he added pointedly. "Cooking with Devon, when I could have been sleeping with Natasha. The man's a disaster, Kerrigan. You should walk the other way."

"A toll bridge?" she repeated with just as much confusion. "Wait—you helped him cook?"

"Yeah, because you married an idiot who doesn't know how to properly identify celery. I'm serious, Rae. I think something might be wrong with him."

"What are you *talking* about?" she repeated. "Devon's a great cook."

"He's not," the assassin replied flatly. "He's been lying to you for years."

And how on earth have you not picked up on it by now?

She laughed, trailing her fingers through her hair.

"He and Julian did this cooking class together in Budapest. Jules got kicked out when he set the carbonator on fire, but the instructor said Devon was the best he'd ever seen."

Gabriel stared in shock, unable to process this.

Why in the world would he...?

"I heard you put Alex in charge of those new transfers," she continued, peering up at him in the pale light. It was like standing by a fire, little waves of heat kept radiating from her hands. "That was a good call." She grinned, giving him a little shove. "You're good at this, Gabriel."

He shoved her in return. "I know."

She was still laughing when Molly summoned her with a bolt of lightning, gesturing furiously to the layer of frost that was accumulating on the wine. "Duty calls."

He waved her off with a grin, running her words through his head.

Yes, he was good was good at his job. But in the end, what did it matter? He was good at a lot of things. He just wasn't sure they were things he wanted to do.

A plume of smoke rose up from the grill, and he turned his eyes to Devon.

Cooking class in Budapest, huh...?

"Hey," he called, strolling across the grass to join him. "We spent nineteen hours in the kitchen on jambalaya. Now you're making hamburgers instead?"

He gestured hopelessly with the spatula. "Molly asked for a little variety. Said she's on some kind of cleanse...?"

I don't think she meant burgers.

"So listen," Gabriel continued, leaning casually against the side of the house, "I was wondering if you could take me to the gun range."

Devon flashed him a look, poking at the grill. "What?"

"The gun range," the assassin repeated, "I was hoping you could take me. You see, Natasha and I have an anniversary coming up, but I don't really know my way around a firearm. I was hoping you might give me a few tips?" The fox's cheeks flamed with a blush, while Gabriel cocked his head with a secret smile. "How to load the barrel, the right way to hold the grip." He ticked them off on his fingers, one after another. "Do you happen to know if there's something called a safety?"

Devon sighed, setting down the spatula. "I saw in the paper that St. Stephen's was re-opening today," he said softly. "I thought it might help to have a little distraction."

Gabriel pursed his lips, fighting back a smile. "We couldn't have watched a match? Or cricket? Anything else but cook?"

"DINNER'S READY!"

The friends gathered together in the middle of the yard—settling into chairs around a single patch of sunlit grass, while the rest of the city battled sleet and fog. The burgers were served and the jambalaya was spooned into great steaming bowls. They had just barely gotten started, when the door swung open a final time and a lovely woman stepped into the yard.

"Since when do these things start on time?" she called.

Angel.

Gabriel was on his feet before he could stop himself, sweeping across the grass in a few long strides, and lifting her straight off her feet. The others shared a secret smile and went back to their conversation, but the assassin was lost in his own world. He hadn't realized how much he'd needed to see her, but it had been gnawing away at him, ever since he walked up the safe house steps.

"I heard you went to the safe house," she said quietly when he finally set her back on the ground. He nodded, and they fell silent. "You didn't happen to see my hairbrush, did you?"

A burst of laughter escaped his lips. "What in the world is wrong with you?" he asked.

She shrugged with a little smile. "I had bad role models." Her eyes swept him up and down, silently assessing. "I also heard you nearly lost your job to a fallen power line. You should be careful with those things."

His eyes flashed involuntarily to Devon. "Yeah, I heard that too."

She followed his gaze, staring thoughtfully. "He's a good guy," she said abruptly.

He glanced down at her in surprise. "...yeah?"

Their eyes met for a moment, then she flashed a wicked smile.

"That's exactly the kind of thing I've been saying to him—watch this. Hey, Devon," she called across the yard, waving for his attention. "That's a great shirt!"

He glanced down without thinking. "Thanks, it's actually—" He caught himself a moment later. "*Stop* trying to be nice to me! It's never going to work!"

She beamed back at him. "Really brings out the magisterial brilliance in your eyes."

The fox flipped her off, while Gabriel shook with silent laughter.

Magisterial brilliance.

The two headed over to the table, taking a seat at the end. A spirited discussion was already in progress, but none of the participants seemed to be making any headway. In fact, they seemed increasingly frustrated the longer it carried on.

"—just doesn't make any sense," Molly was saying. "Why would he make us break into a museum and find this secret metal, only to discover that we couldn't move it off the plate? Just to get us arrested? There are way easier ways to get us arrested than that."

Angel flashed a curious look, and Gabriel leaned closer.

"I forgot to tell you, the statue was on a pressure plate."

"Maybe we missed something," Luke said with a shrug. "Maybe he just thought it would be funny if we got carted away from the British Museum. He's always hated that place, ever since they gave him a lifetime ban."

"I don't know why we're still talking about him," Rae muttered, jabbing a fork into her jambalaya. "Last year for Christmas, he sent me a pitchfork and a potato-gun."

James perked up from the other side of the table. "Do you still have it?"

"He wouldn't have sent us in there for no reason," Devon interjected, circling them back on task. A part of him was desperate to write the whole thing off as another one of Kraigan Kerrigan's famous misadventures, but he couldn't let it rest. "It has to be something to do with the clue. He told us to open her tomb, he told us to pry off the metal—"

"—which showed us the tambor," Julian finished, "but that isn't enough to lead us to the next clue. It's a rare metal, but there's nothing particularly mysterious about it, and we've already secured the other two locations. So why tell us? And why cover the thing in gold?"

The table fell silent, as each of them wondered the same thing.

"It isn't about the gold," Angel murmured. "He told you to peel away the gold. It's about the tambor. How much did the statue weigh?" she asked abruptly. "I'm assuming you guys had a read on the pressure plate. How much did it weigh when you peeled away the gold—*precisely*?"

Luke pulled a phone from his pocket, pulling up his history.

"Eighteen thousand, five hundred and forty-seven pounds."

The number dropped like a stone between them.

"Does that mean something?" Molly asked. "Is that number significant somehow?"

All eyes turned to Angel.

"I'm not sure," she answered pensively, lips curving with a smile. "But I know someone who might be able to figure it out…"

THE END

President on Edge Blurb

CAREFUL PULLING ON threads, you never know what might unravel...

When Kraigan's latest clue leads to the most unlikely of places, the Kerrigan Gang is forced to consider how far they're willing to stretch to solve the mystery of his abduction. But things have taken a turn in London, and a series of dark coincidences makes them wonder if the circumstances of his kidnapping are more serious than they first appeared.

Tensions are brewing between the Council and the Knights. A brush with the shadow organization leaves one person dead, and one in the hospital. The gang comes together to finish them once and for all, but the arrival of a mysterious package changes everything.

Could the two cases be linked? Could Kraigan be in trouble after all?

Are they already too late...?

PRESIDENT
W.J. MAY
GET IT ON
Google Play
kobo
Available at
amazon
nook

Kerrigan Presidents Series

Leaders in Control
Director on a Mission
Devon Seeking Guidance
Gabriel Vanishing Light
President on Edge
Agreeing the Future

Kerrigan Memoirs Series

The Chronicles of:
Devon
Angel
Julian
Molly
Gabriel
Rae

The Kerrigan Kids Series

Book 1 - School of Potential
Book 2 - Myths & Magic
Book 3 - Kith & Kin
Book 4 - Playing With Power
Book 5 - Line of Ancestry
Book 6 - Descent of Hope
Book 7 – Illusion of Shadows
Book 8 – Frozen by the Future
Book 9 – Guilt of My Past
Book 10 – Demise of Magic
Book 11- Rise of the Prophecy
Book 12 – Deafened by the Past

TUDOR COMPARISON:

Aumbry Hall – A recess to hold sacred vessels, often found in castle chapels.

Aumbry House was considered very special to hold the female students - their sacred vessels (especially Rae Kerrigan).

Joist Hall – A timber stretched from wall-to-wall to support floorboards.

Joist House was considered a building of support where the male students could support and help each other.

Oratory – A private chapel in a house.

Private education room in the school where the students were able to practice their gifting and improve their skills. Also used as a banquet - dance hall when needed.

Oriel – A projecting window in a wall; originally a form of porch, often of wood. The original bay windows of the Tudor period. Guilder College majority of windows were oriel.

Rae often felt her life was being watching through one of these windows. Hence the constant reference to them.

Refectory – A communal dining hall. Same termed used in Tudor times.

Scriptorium – A Medieval writing room in which scrolls were also housed.

Used for English classes and still store some of the older books from the Tudor reign (regarding tatùs).

Privy Council –Secret council and "arm of the government" similar to the CIA, etc.... In Tudor times, the Privy Council was King Henry's board of advisors and helped run the country.

Find W.J. May

Website:
https://www.wjmaybooks.com
Facebook:
https://www.facebook.com/pages/Author-WJ-May-FAN-PAGE/141170442608149
Newsletter:
SIGN UP FOR W.J. May's Newsletter to find out about new releases, updates, cover reveals and even freebies!
http://www.wjmaybooks.com/subscribe

The Chronicles of Kerrigan
BOOK I - *Rae of Hope* is FREE!
Book Trailer:
http://www.youtube.com/watch?v=gILAwXxx8MU
Book II - *Dark Nebula*
Book Trailer:
http://www.youtube.com/watch?v=Ca24STi_bFM
Book III - *House of Cards*
Book IV - *Royal Tea*
Book V - *Under Fire*
Book VI - *End in Sight*
Book VII – *Hidden Darkness*
Book VIII – *Twisted Together*
Book IX – *Mark of Fate*
Book X – *Strength & Power*
Book XI – *Last One Standing*
BOOK XII – *Rae of Light*

PREQUEL –
Christmas Before the Magic
Question the Darkness
Into the Darkness
Fight the Darkness
Alone the Darkness
Lost the Darkness

SEQUEL –
**Matter of Time
Time Piece
Second Chance
Glitch in Time
Out Time
Precious Time**

The Chronicles of Kerrigan: Gabriel
Living in the Past

Present for Today

Staring at the Future

More books by W.J. May

Hidden Secrets Saga:
Download Seventh Mark part 1 For FREE
Book Trailer:
http://www.youtube.com/watch?v=Y-_vVYC1gvo

LIKE MOST TEENAGERS, Rouge is trying to figure out who she is and what she wants to be. With little knowledge about her past, she has questions but has never tried to find the answers. Everything changes when she befriends a strangely intoxicating family. Siblings Grace and Michael, appear to have secrets which seem connected to Rouge. Her hunch is confirmed when a horrible incident occurs at an outdoor party. Rouge may be the only one who can find the answer.

An ancient journal, a Sioghra necklace and a special mark force life-altering decisions for a girl who grew up unprepared to fight for her life or others.

All secrets have a cost and Rouge's determination to find the truth can only lead to trouble...or something even more sinister.

Don't miss out!

Visit the website below and you can sign up to receive emails whenever W.J. May publishes a new book. There's no charge and no obligation.

https://books2read.com/r/B-A-SSF-PGMJC

BOOKS 2 READ

Connecting independent readers to independent writers.

Did you love *Gabriel's Vanishing Light*? Then you should read *Adversity*[1] by W.J. May!

They say some people are favored by the gods. Others need to make their own luck.

When Cora wandered out of the woods during a winter storm, she was on the brink of death. Lost in a strange land, with nothing but her unborn child, she threw herself at the mercy of the gods. But her story wasn't finished just yet, and the fates had other plans.

A kindly woman delivers the child safely and gives her the chance to start anew. The troubles of the past are safely buried, a shining future is within reach. When a handsome warrior in the king's guard comes to town a few months later, the two begin to fall madly in love.

---

1. https://books2read.com/u/ml8L6M

2. https://books2read.com/u/ml8L6M

But Cora has a deadly secret. And secrets have a way of coming to light.

Every legend has to start somewhere…

In a time when Vikings clashed against Romans, and whispers of magic held back the tides, a young woman staggered out of the forest and gave birth to a special child...

The Viking Tales

Adversity - the Prequel **Warrior** **Defender** **Contender** **Affinity** **Heroine** **Victory**

Read more at www.wjmaybooks.com.

Also by W.J. May

Beginning's End Series
Beginnings
Curiosity
Scrutiny
Foresight
Disavow
Trickery
Wisdom
Decree
Influence
Prevail
Beginning's End Series Box Set Books #1-3

Blood Red Series
Courage Runs Red
The Night Watch
Marked by Courage
Forever Night
The Other Side of Fear
Blood Red Box Set Books #1-5

Daughters of Darkness: Victoria's Journey
Victoria
Huntress
Coveted (A Vampire & Paranormal Romance)
Twisted
Daughter of Darkness - Victoria - Box Set

Fae Wilds Series
Twist and Turns
Curse of the Fae
Force the Truth
Crown and Glory
Enemy and Rivals
Light in the Dark
Dusk and Shadows
Called by Midnight
Dark Memories

Great Temptation Series
The Devil's Footsteps
Heaven's Command
Mortals Surrender

Hidden Secrets Saga
Seventh Mark - Part 1
Seventh Mark - Part 2

Marked By Destiny
Compelled
Fate's Intervention
Chosen Three
The Hidden Secrets Saga: The Complete Series

Kerrigan Chronicles
Stopping Time
A Passage of Time
Ticking Clock
Secrets in Time
Time in the City
Ultimate Future

Kerrigan Memoirs
Chronicles of Devon
Chronicles of Angel
Chronicles of Julian
Chronicles of Molly
Chronicles of Gabriel
Chronicles of Rae

Kerrigan Presidents Series
Leaders in Control
Director on a Mission
Devon Seeking Guidance
Gabriel's Vanishing Light
President on Edge

Mending Magic Series
Lost Souls
Illusion of Power
Challenging the Dark
Castle of Power
Limits of Magic
Protectors of Light
Mending Magic Box Set Books #1-3

Omega Queen Series
Discipline
Bravery
Courage
Conquer
Strength
Validation
Approval
Blessing
Balance
Grievance
Enchanted
Gratified
Omega Queen - Box Set Books #1-3

Paranormal Huntress Series
Never Look Back
Coven Master
Alpha's Permission

Blood Bonding
Oracle of Nightmares
Shadows in the Night
Paranormal Huntress BOX SET

Prophecy Series
Only the Beginning
White Winter
Secrets of Destiny

Revamped Series
Hidden
Banished
Converted

Royal Factions
The Price For Peace
The Cost for Surviving
The Punishment For Deception
Faking Perfection
The Most Cherished
The Strength to Endure
Royal Factions Box Set Books #1-3

Royal Guard Series
Guardian

Paladin
Sentinel
Royal Guard Box Set

The Chronicles of Kerrigan
Rae of Hope
Dark Nebula
House of Cards
Royal Tea
Under Fire
End in Sight
Hidden Darkness
Twisted Together
Mark of Fate
Strength & Power
Last One Standing
Rae of Light
The Chronicles of Kerrigan Box Set Books # 1 - 6

The Chronicles of Kerrigan: Gabriel
Living in the Past
Present For Today
Staring at the Future

The Chronicles of Kerrigan Prequel
Christmas Before the Magic
Question the Darkness
Into the Darkness

Fight the Darkness
Alone in the Darkness
Lost in Darkness
The Chronicles of Kerrigan Prequel Series Books #1-3

The Chronicles of Kerrigan Sequel
A Matter of Time
Time Piece
Second Chance
Glitch in Time
Our Time
Precious Time

The Hidden Secrets Saga
Seventh Mark (part 1 & 2)

The Kerrigan Kids
School of Potential
Myths & Magic
Kith & Kin
Playing With Power
Line of Ancestry
Descent of Hope
Illusion of Shadows
Frozen by the Future
Guilt Of My Past
Demise of Magic
Rise of The Prophecy

Deafened By The Past
The Kerrigan Kids Box Set Books #1-3

The Queen's Alpha Series
Eternal
Everlasting
Unceasing
Evermore
Forever
Boundless
Prophecy
Protected
Foretelling
Revelation
Betrayal
Resolved
The Queen's Alpha Box Set

The Senseless Series
Radium Halos - Part 1
Radium Halos - Part 2
Nonsense
Perception
The Senseless - Box Set Books #1-4

The Viking Tales
Adversity

Standalone
Shadow of Doubt (Part 1 & 2)
Five Shades of Fantasy
Zwarte Nevel
Shadow of Doubt - Part 1
Shadow of Doubt - Part 2
Four and a Half Shades of Fantasy
Dream Fighter
What Creeps in the Night
Forest of the Forbidden
Arcane Forest: A Fantasy Anthology
The First Fantasy Box Set

Watch for more at www.wjmaybooks.com.

About the Author

About W.J. May

Welcome to USA TODAY BESTSELLING author W.J. May's Page! SIGN UP for W.J. May's Newsletter to find out about new releases, updates, cover reveals and even freebies! http://eepurl.com/97aYf

Website: http://www.wjmaybooks.com

Facebook: http://www.facebook.com/pages/Author-WJ-May-FAN-PAGE/141170442608149?ref=hl *Please feel free to connect with me and share your comments. I love connecting with my readers.*

W.J. May grew up in the fruit belt of Ontario. Crazy-happy childhood, she always has had a vivid imagination and loads of energy. After her father passed away in 2008, from a six-year battle with cancer (which she still believes he won the fight against), she began to write again. A passion she'd loved for years, but realized life was too short to keep putting it off. She is a writer of Young Adult, Fantasy Fiction and where ever else her little muses take her.

Read more at www.wjmaybooks.com.

Made in the USA
Columbia, SC
10 July 2025